IN BOUNDS

GARNET DAVENPORT

For the girls who not only want the guy with abs...
but also the career

ZERI WILLIAMS

*Y*ou know, all I wanted to do was relax on the last day of the year before I went out with my sister to bring in the new year. However, my new job as PR Manager for the Pittsburgh Scavengers was already taking over my life. I wasn't officially on the job. I was supposed to be learning the team, working with sponsors, and setting up public appearances. Let's not forget getting to know what everyone's social media accounts were like and who needed to be 'handled' more than the others.

All that changed in a matter of minutes.

"Zeri, I'd like for you to be at this club... ummm... I just had the name right here."

I heard a bunch of papers shuffle around on what I presumed to be the giant desk in his office where I accepted my very first corporate job for the Pittsburgh Scavengers from the owner, Bill Conway. This man made his billions, yes, billions with a b, from everything. Oil, yes. Real estate, yes. Insurance, yes. Was he a bad guy? No. But he wasn't going to apologize for how he got to where he was—the point zero zero one of America's wealthiest men. However, the reason I say he's not so bad is because he turns around, pays his people well, gives fantastic benefits, donates profits to charities, and has always been a down to earth kind of guy. To top all of that off, I heard he's got a whole slew of daughters. The man's been through enough.

"Got it," he called out in victory. "Double Down. I've been informed many of my players will be there tonight. With it being New Year's Eve, I would just like to make sure that my boys don't get into trouble."

I wasn't sure exactly how I was supposed to accomplish that, considering that none of them knew who I was.

Before I could say anything, Bill continued. "Zeri, this is one reason I hired you. You know the best ways to get into and out of situations." He chuckled, probably remembering my interview.

I found out that he was hiring for the prime position of PR Manager. I mean, how could I have passed up the opportunity? So, without an interview scheduled, I snuck into Conway Corporate offices and finagled my way up to the twenty-first floor for an unscheduled interview. When I strutted into Bill Conway's office and told him what I was doing there and how I got in, we talked for over two hours, and he offered me the job on the spot. Said he loved my charisma and gumption.

"I know," I said, agreeing with him. "I've got your back."

"I know you do. Just make sure none of my boys end up doing anything they'll regret," Bill said.

"I can't keep whoever is there from ending up in the tabloids, but I can go and introduce myself so they know someone is there watching them."

A booming laugh came out of Bill that was typical of our conversations.

"I bet you'll do just fine. I've dropped your name at the door and given you a plus one," he said.

"Yes, sir."

"Good, I will see you in the office this next week for your official first day," he said just before he hung up.

"He'll always be to the point," I said to myself, looking at my phone.

I walked out of my room to make sure my sister was up and checked her Retriever app for her jobs for the day. I may have gotten an advance to get us to Pittsburgh, but it was going quick.

"Sou, you up yet?" I called out.

I love my sister to the end of the world, but she could sleep like the dead sometimes. I looked around our tiny one bedroom loft and then up to the loft. It was the smallest room. Sou decided to take it since she wasn't going to be able to put the same amount toward our rent. All she had up there was a twin bed, three-drawer dresser she had painted yellow when we were kids, and a clothes rack. Other than that, there was maybe three square feet of walking space and then the spiral staircase that led straight into the kitchen. Behind the kitchen was our bathroom. The living room was big enough for a loveseat and small entertainment unit from IKEA, and my room was just on the other side of that. Not huge but at least there was a window and closet. I even had enough room to put a desk and chair so I could do some work from home as needed. I also had a full size bed in my room.

"Sou?" I called out again as I started going up the stairs to the loft. "Sou, you've got to get up. It's almost eight."

"Mmm... I'm up." She moaned without opening her eyes.

"No, you're not. You've got to get up."

"Fine, Mom, I'm up," she whined as she sat up and started to stretch her muscles to help them wake up.

"Don't call me Mom. She would have brought you breakfast in bed," I replied, picking up her clothes from the night before off the floor.

"That's right, where's my vanilla latte?"

"Oh, down in the kitchen..."

"Really?" she asked excitedly.

"No. You're going to have to make it yourself. But I do have some good news."

"What?" she asked flatly.

"We're going to go to Double Down tonight for their New Year's Eve party."

"What? Really? How'd you swing that?" she asked getting out of bed and starting her way down the stairs so that she could take her time in the bathroom.

"The Scavengers hooked us up."

"That's freaking badass," she called out through the door of the bathroom. "I should be done with everything early enough to get back here and put something sexy on."

"I've got a thing after lunch, but I should be back with plenty of time to get ready with you and then we'll go."

"This made my day. Whoever did this is awesome. I've been wanting to hit up Double Down since we moved. But between everything and work, I never thought I'd get there and to be on the list."

"Are you being serious? It's just a club," I said.

She swung open the bathroom door to look me directly in the eye. "It's not just a club. It's a club owned by a professional athlete."

"What? No," I said, taking out my phone and starting my search.

There it was in black and white. Phoenix Drayden was co-owner of Double Down. He's been the co-owner for like five years. How did I not know this? Phoenix Drayden was huge news when he married longtime girlfriend Chloe Summers at the beginning of the year. Her father was a political goldmine before his scandal hit all media outlets. That PR manager was on point. Handled that like a goddamn pro. It all went away in a few months. When Drayden moved to Pittsburgh for the Badgers, his girlfriend followed, and every bit of rumor attached was gone. There was still fallout and fans were upset, but it could have been way worse.

"I told ya," she said as she walked past me into the kitchen to put a pod into the machine.

She got her favorite green and orange coffee mug and then pulled mine out.

"Nope, I don't have time. I'm just going to grab a hot tea out somewhere," I replied.

"Okay. I'll see you later. It looks like I've got five jobs then I have a meeting with my manager," she said.

"Anything to be worried about?" I asked.

I've never been invited to speak to a manager without it being something bad. In fact, one time when I worked in a drug store, the store manager had pulled me in while I was there just grabbing a drink on my way out to write me up. Over something that wasn't even my fault. I had worked as a technician in the pharmacy, and I couldn't hear the last name of the customer through the drive thru. The pharmacist came over and typed in the name she heard, pulled the script, and I sold it. It was the wrong prescription. But I hadn't known. It was my first time working in the drive thru and the first time I was the only registered technician on duty. I normally was in the photo lab, and I'd only been used as extra coverage. Well, it was my fault, and I decided that even though the pharmacist handed me the wrong prescription to sell, it was on me. So I took the write-up and learned from my mistake. That was the last time I ever didn't double check even people over me. Because of my attention to details and figuring out problems, I excelled in public relations in high school and college. Now at nearly twenty-six, I feel like I've lived a lifetime.

"Nah, I've gotten five stars with each job. My clients love me," she said as she moved past me to go back up to her loft.

I received a notification on my phone.

James: I'm horny. When are you going to get here?

Gah. Why does he have to be so crass? Was I still going to go? Yes. Good dick is good dick. And I orgasmed some of the time.

It was just easier to keep him around than to find a new guy to have a no strings attached relationship with.

Me: I'm getting ready now.

Those three little dots started moving. I went into my room and started pulling out everything I needed to put on. I'd put on this gold lingerie set I got for myself last year. James and I have been "seeing" each other since the first weekend I moved to Pittsburgh. He's nothing exceptional, and we're not serious, but we get together two or three times a week to wear each other out in the best ways possible. And honestly, his personality is a lot sometimes. He only likes things his way, and he moves through people like coffee pods. I'm sure I'm not the only one he's "seeing" this week.

I put on my outfit and put on the littlest amount of makeup. I didn't want to put on so much that I would just sweat it off. And I obviously didn't want Soumaya to know I was spending time in the afternoons to meet a man for sex. How barbaric. Gasp.

She sees me as the responsible one. Our parents expect that I will be able to manage both of us. But I'd rather just spend one day with zero responsibilities and live off the ecstasy of life.

LUTHER 'ZEUS' ZEUSES

"*Y*ou're going to be there tonight, right?" I asked my best friend, Dominic D'Angelo.

Dom's been my best friend since we were basically in diapers. Technically, my mom worked for his mom, but they were really good friends past the professional one. When my mom came to the D'Angelo's house to clean twice a week, she'd bring me. Dom and I would sit on the couch and give each other the answers to every question on our math homework.

"I told you I'd be there, and I will. I can't let you get all the pussy," he teased back.

I had been hydrating the entire day to prepare myself for New Year's Eve. Double Down was the place to be, and I had made sure that I had VIP access and prime pussy waiting for me. There are some regulars at the club that get invited into VIP who keep their mouths shut about what happens behind the black and gold curtain.

I got to Double Down early enough to grease a few palms and see Nix Drayden before he took off with his lovely wife, who looked like she just got fucked in the back room. She had come from the back adjusting her top while Nix made sure we would be taken care of for the night.

"Is there anything you need?" Nix asked.

"No, we'll be great. Thanks, man," I said.

"Of course, anything for a friend. But I'm going to take my wife and get home to our son," Nix said as his wife, Chloe, came up behind him and put her arm around him. He naturally moved his arm around her so that she tucked perfectly into him.

Fuck me, that's cute.

After Nix and his wife left, I went up to the VIP section and sat on the red leather sofa. I felt like a god. My arms lying across the back and my legs laid wide. I was ready.

"Sir, is there anything I can get you?" the security, Sterling, assigned to our VIP room asked.

"Nah, I'm good. I don't want to get my drink on until my boys get here."

"Yes, sir."

As the night turned darker, more and more of my team presented themselves for a night of fun and debauchery. The moment two of the finest women I've seen walked through the curtain, my cock stood up and took notice. Barely-there miniskirts and tops, dresses that didn't leave anything to the imagination, and skin everywhere. Skin I wanted to get my hands on. Each woman escorted into the VIP room was a different shade of beautiful.

I walked over and leaned in beside one of them wearing a silver scrap of polyester. "Dance?" I said, holding out my hand for hers.

"Can my friend join?" she said in an annoying nasally voice that reminded me of Fran on *The Nanny*.

At least with the music and dancing, I won't have to hear her speak. I like those seductive voices that purr when she speaks.

I gave her a panty-melting smirk and reached out my other hand for her friend. As the beat started to pulse, both of the women started to grind against me. Not a bad way to go if I do say so myself. The woman with the nasally voice was wearing a silver miniskirt with matching top that was held over her breasts by a string and knot—my favorite kind. Her hair was pulled back away from her fully painted face, and her hoop earrings could possibly fit around her neck; they were so big. Her friend was in a hot pink mini dress. No way she could be wearing anything under it. Her natural black hair was short against her head with a little bit of length at the top. Both were wearing heels that made them at least four inches taller. Good for me. At six-six, I'm not short, and I want a woman that can give me an athlete baby. Nothing against those little five-four cuties, but I felt like I could break them in half when we fuck.

I didn't like all that fakeness either. At least the woman wearing the pink dress wasn't wearing so much makeup that it changed how she appeared. Very natural with the slightest of cat's eye with her mascara.

"Yo! Dom, get your ass over here," I called out as soon as my eyes met his.

He came over to join us. The woman I hadn't heard speak started to focus on Dom. We let them grind on us through the next couple of songs. I didn't mind. The girl in the silver was definitely fuckable.

I tilted my head over the balcony of the VIP room we were in to see all the bodies on the floor. I caught sight of a woman who piqued my interest immediately. Her black dress hugged her curves, and she was showing the slightest cleavage on display. She was gorgeous. I needed to get closer to her. I made the decision at that moment she would be my kiss at midnight.

I noticed Dom had a very similar reaction to her as I did. My man deserved at least to have a shot. But there's no way she would pick him when she could have me.

Dom walked off. The girl in the hot pink mini dress nearly fell over. I helped to make sure she didn't land on her ass as I watched Dom walk out of the VIP. He was really going to try to introduce himself to her. I slowed my grinding with the girl, who basically had her ass on my dick, to watch what would happen.

He started getting closer and closer to my target. I had stopped dancing with the girls at this point. They didn't even care. They just started dancing with each other. I'd probably have a better night if I just walked away from a possible threesome and went home alone.

I spread my arms out on the banister railing and glared. I wanted to punch my best friend for even speaking with the woman I was interested in. The only good part was she didn't look interested in him at all. I caught a waitress walking by with a glass of amber liquid on a tray. I snatched it and threw it back in one swift gulp.

Wincing from the heat, I set the glass down on the nearest table and made my way around the room to get down to the floor level. I'm moving through the crowd as the clock inched its way close to midnight.

Our eyes met a few times as I made my way toward her. There was an attraction happening. The girl she was there with leaned in to speak into her ear and then walked away.

"TEN!" everyone called out.

"NINE!"

I was just a few feet away.

"EIGHT!"

"SEVEN!"

I was readying myself for my hands to be all over her gorgeous body.

"SIX!"

"FIVE, FOUR, THREE..."

I pulled her close.

"TWO!"

There wasn't even time for one word.

"ONE!"

"HAPPY NEW YEAR!"

Her skin was soft and smooth. The heat was coming off her

like fire. I dipped my head down to hers, our mouth met in celebration, and she tasted like an apple martini. I wanted to keep tasting her, but she pulled away when I wanted to keep kissing.

"Wait..." I said.

"I've got to find my sister," she said, looking around.

"Your sister?" I asked, confused.

"Yeah, she was just here."

"Let's just get a table, and she can come find you," I offered, seeing a table unoccupied.

She was almost thinking about it for a moment, but she turned around to keep looking. There was no way I'd get her attention with her sister missing.

"I've really got to find her," she said as she took off.

Girl was quick. She was right in front of me one moment, and then the next she was gone. It was as if she vanished into thin air. I looked everywhere for her. When I couldn't find her on the floor, I went over to the bar to ask the bartender if he had any information on the girl.

"There was a woman in here..."

"Man, there's been a lot of women in here," he said as he pulled another glass of beer for a customer. "I wouldn't be able to tell you."

I nodded. "Thanks, man," I said, tapping my knuckle on the bar top and then walking off to see if I could find my mystery woman.

ZERI WILLIAMS

"*H*arder!" I said, digging my nails into James' muscular bareback as he thrust into me from behind.

It hadn't taken more than two seconds of me coming into this corporate office for James to close the blinds and start removing my clothes. He had sent his assistant off and forwarded all his calls to voicemail just as he normally had prepared for me. No interruptions.

His fingers gripped onto my hips as he pulled out then slammed back in.

"Fuck." He hissed.

His wood desk was cold beneath my breasts, making my nipples pucker, and my skin more sensitive to the touch. He liked me bent over his desk. He liked to slap my ass. I didn't mind it. He knew what he was doing.

"Deeper!" I ordered.

"I'm balls deep. There is not a deeper," he snapped as he slammed his hips against my ass twice and then spanked my hip with his right hand.

I winced. That would leave a handprint. The sensation made my walls tense and tighten around his dick.

"Fuck, yes, baby. That feels so good." James groaned.

That's all it took. My orgasm started at my core and sent waves of pleasure through my body. He thrust into me one last time before his own orgasmic grunts came. As we both let our orgasms wean down, we breathed heavily onto each other.

"That was exactly what I needed." He panted then pulled out, took off the condom to throw away, and started to buckle his pants.

I pushed myself up from the desk. With my breasts exposed, I maneuvered them back inside their gold lace prison and bent down to pick up my fitted skirt and button up silk top. I had gotten it in a secondhand shop and was as giddy as I could be that it was in fabulous condition.

"Can I see you tonight?" he asked.

"No. I've got plans with my sister."

"Fine." He huffed.

He hated not getting his way. I probably should end whatever relationship there is before he tries to claim me.

"I'm sure you won't be lonely tonight," I said.

"No, I won't," he said. "You can leave now."

"I plan on it," I said, buttoning the last button and tucking in my top, then walking out of his office.

His assistant was at her desk. I hadn't even cared if she heard. It was good sex, and it was all done in private. Even if it was in his office. I met James McThatton in a coffee shop after he met with a client. I accidentally bumped into him, and we started a conversation. He would always be bound by attorney client privilege. He knows his way around the law, and it came in handy when I needed to run through my new contract. He was more than happy to make sure I was getting the best deal— and I was.

I nodded as I walked by. She knew exactly why we were in his office. I'd have to meet him somewhere else next time. He didn't like for us to meet at his apartment. I wasn't surprised.

He didn't seem like the kind of man that liked a woman in his personal space.

I was all the way across town. It would take me over an hour to get home. I decided to check in with my sister to make sure everything was still on for Double Down. I pressed her number and waited for the Bluetooth to connect.

"You're still coming tonight, right?" I asked.

"Yeah, of course. I'm just leaving work now," Soumaya said.

"Thank God, hey, don't forget to put your Do Not Disturb on in the app."

"Right, thanks," she said.

"What are you going to wear tonight? Please don't tell me you don't have anything," I said.

"No, I have something. You remember that purple dress?"

"Oh yeah, the one with long sleeves that looks amazing on you?" I replied.

"That's the one," Soumaya said.

"Can I borrow those silver heels with the rhinestones?" I asked.

"Yeah, I was going to ask if I could borrow Mom's good luck earrings," she said.

"Of course."

"Thanks."

"It will be fine. You're the best *you-wreck-it-I'll-fix-it* chick in the business."

I giggled. Maybe I was the *you-wreck-it-I'll-fix-it* chick. I kind of liked that title more. I was good at my job, and I loved handling people to help them in their lives. Just about everywhere I sent my resume said I wasn't old enough to have the experience needed to handle their clients. That was why when I heard the Scavengers were looking for a new public relations manager, I jumped on the opportunity to knock their socks off. I loved that I didn't have to worry about getting more clients, and clients from all over the map made my job easier. I worked for the team. Protect the team's image.

"Thanks, but I'm going to be meeting some of the team tonight, and I wanted to make a good impression," I explained.

"And you will. You're going to knock those Neanderthals on their asses with your skills."

"You don't know how much I needed to hear that," I said, taking a deep breath.

"I know. You didn't need to hear it, but sometimes it's just nice to have it said."

"You're right. I'll see you at home in a bit?"

"Yep, I'm on my way now," she replied.

I had just enough time to stop by my favorite secondhand shop to see if I could find something extra for tonight. I pulled into the parking lot of *Once Upon a Second Chance*. I loved the little ship that looked like a fairy tale from the time you walked through the front door until you left. I opened the door to the twinkling of the shop door bells. The purple walls with gold accents and butterflies was my favorite part.

"Welcome to Once Upon a Second Chance. Let me know if you need any help finding anything," the girl behind the desk said.

"Thank you," I said as I went right to the evening wear rack.

With every scratch of the metal hanger against the metal rack, hope started to fizzle out. I just needed something simple.

Swipe. Scratch.

Swipe. Scratch.

Swipe. Scratch.

I was almost at the end where the little plastic sizer goes to the next size up when I spotted it. Solid black with long sleeves and a swooped v-neck. I pulled it from the rack to double check the size and got excited.

"I just need to try this on," I said to the girl.

"Sure," she said, grabbing the keys and taking me back to the dressing rooms. "I always like being in the back. The mirrors are so much better."

"Thank you."

I went into the dressing room and started the process of seeing how it looked on me. Turning and checking out all the areas I normally feel self-conscious about. I'd never tell my sister that there's anything about myself I didn't like. It would be like me talking right about her. It looked pretty cute. A little low in the front, but it was a decent length. I checked the tags. *Sacks Fifth Avenue*. Score.

I changed out of it and sat down on the small bench inside the dressing room to check over the fabric to make sure that there were no rips or tears. I hadn't even put my clothes back on when the girl came back to knock on the door.

"You okay in there?"

"Yes, thank you," I said, putting my clothes back on and then taking the dress to the register counter.

"Didn't you have another dress too?" she asked, eyeing me as if I walked in ready to be a thief.

"No," I said loud and firmly.

The owner came out from the curtain in the back looking directly at me. "Zeri, Babe, you're looking great. How are you?"

"Thanks, Kaitlyn, I'm great," I said, looking back at the girl who all but accused me of stealing a dress I never picked up.

"Kaitlyn, I think she had another dress when she went into the dressing room, but she only came out with this one."

"Oh!" She said, looking nervous, "Zeri is one of my best customers."

"Then you know that this might not be the only time she's concealed other items to walk out with them," she said with a tone of superiority.

I narrowed my eyes on the girl.

I'd done nothing wrong, and she knew it. How dare she accuse me of stealing from Kaitlyn. I would never steal. However, this wasn't the first time I'd been accused, and I was sure it wasn't going to be the last. You know that scene in *Pretty Woman* where Vivian goes into the shop and the bitch tells her that she can't purchase anything because of the way she looks?

That's what it is like to do anything in cities where any person of color is labeled as a criminal.

"No," Kaitlyn snapped.

"But—" the girl started.

"No. I'm not going to hear this. Go into the office. I will meet you there when I am done here." She turned to me and said, "I am so sorry, Zeri."

Kaitlyn extended her arms for the dress and went to the register to scan the Once Upon a Second Chance blue tag. When she tapped on the screen, I noticed the price change by twenty dollars.

"I am so sorry. I promise this will not happen again. I don't hire people that discriminate," Kaitlyn explained. "I added a discount. Please don't think that everyone is like that here."

"I know, Kaitlyn. I've never had any issues before here," I told her.

"I am glad to hear that and don't worry, this will not happen again."

I paid as she packaged my dress in pink tissue paper and put it into a black paper gift bag. Kaitlyn took care with everything she was doing to make sure I left with an exceptional experience past her employee. She stapled a ten dollar gift certificate to my receipt and then handed it to me.

"Again, I am so sorry she did that."

"I know she doesn't represent you, but she does represent your shop," I said.

"I know. I'm so sorry."

I nodded and hoped she would do what she needed to do to retain the non-discrimination environment they'd done so well keeping until now. I wouldn't want to not support a small business that does what's right to keep a great staff.

I got back out to my car and put the bag into the passenger seat with my clutch. I was nearly an hour away from home with traffic, and it was only getting worse. Turning on Bruno Mars and trying to stay calm as the population of Pittsburgh was out on the road either on their way home to get ready for midnight or already on their way out.

I was running so late by the time I pulled into the parking lot at our little historic walk-up. I checked the time, seeing that we would need to get going so we could make it there before ten. I just kept reminding myself of everything I needed to get done before we could leave.

ZERI WILLIAMS

"Hey Z," she said as she finished off her glass of wine.

"God," I sighed, "I'm running so far behind. Give me five minutes."

"You're going to need more than five minutes," she called out.

"Don't," I snapped at her, not needing the reminder that I was running behind and I was never the one that needed to hurry.

"Whaaat?" she said, raising her hands into the air.

"You know what. It's been a long day, and I've got to get through tonight without any problems," I said, making sure she understood I didn't need her to add to my stress the way she normally did.

"I said nothing. Just take your time. It's not like they're even expecting you," she said.

"I know, but I need to be there," I called out from my room as I changed. I knew I really didn't have to be there, but I should make an appearance since it was brought up by my boss. "I told you I'd be done in five." I was wearing a new-to-me gorgeous black dress that hugged my curves. I loved it even more than I had in the store. But the emotion that came with what happened to me was still there. I tried to push it down and move forward, but more than likely, I'd end up getting rid of the dress out of principle.

"Damn, Sis, check you out. When did you get that?" she asked.

"I just got it," I said, giving her a spin. "It will go perfect with those silver rhinestone heels."

"Right, let me grab them."

She went up to her loft area while I double checked myself in the small mirror I had in my makeup compact. On her way back down, she said, "Did you grab Mom's earrings?"

"Oh, yeah," I said, going back into my room and digging into my jewelry box sitting on my dresser.

I traded her earrings for heels and then fingered them onto my feet. The strap hooking behind my heel and making sure they were fastened well.

"You look so good," I said, eyeing her through the small mirror.

"You're not so bad yourself. We look good." She said, "Are you ready to get it?"

"You bet."

I made arrangements to take a Lyft to Double Down. I hadn't wanted us to drink even one drink and have to wonder about the car. When our Lyft driver dropped us off at Double Down, I went up to the bouncer to give him my name. We were able to get in without any wait whatsoever.

Inside, we locked arms with each other in comfort and made our way through the crowd.

"I'm going to get us drinks," I said, nodding toward the bar.

She pointed over toward an area where there were less people. I nodded knowing exactly what she was wanting. We didn't mind being around people, but we wanted to have a little space especially if we were going to start drinking.

"Two apple martinis, please," I said speaking loud enough for the bartender to hear.

He nodded. "ID?"

I nodded, opening my clutch and showing my ID. It was a twenty-one and older club, but one thing I had heard was that you will get your ID checked several times. All the employees were trained to identify fake IDs.

"Hey, we meet again." A gruff voice spoke right into my ear causing a weird chill to cover my entire body.

I spun around to come face to face with an extremely tall, attractive man that looked familiar, but I just couldn't place him.

"Uh, hi?" I said.

"I didn't think I was going to see you again. Did you wanna get out of here?" he asked.

"No. I don't know you," I said, confused.

"Yeah, we met at my sister's house. You flirted with me," he encouraged.

"I don't know what you are talking about," I said, wanting him to go away.

There was something about him that put me off completely. He was certainly attractive, but there was something about him that made me want to run in the other direction. I turned back around once he got the message. I eased the moment he walked off.

The bartender checked in with me to make sure I was all right and that the man hadn't pushed too far. I loved that they were attentive to their female customers. There are still people that would put something in your drink just to have a moment alone with an unwilling partner.

There were three other bartenders working on other drinks as he got started mixing. There was no time tonight for a show. The mix went quite easy without a performance. He added in the slightest amount of apple juice. He set the nearly neon green drinks in front of me. They smelled perfectly sour. Finally someone who knew how to make a proper martini. I took a small sip and smiled. The sour and sweet hit my tastebuds with gusto.

"Good?" he asked.

"Yes, very. Thank you," I replied.

He smiled back and nodded before he went to take another drink order. I watched as his toned tush worked its way to another customer and turned around to grab a bottle off the top shelf.

"Nice ass," I hissed to myself.

He turned around and gave me a wink as if he heard me say it.

I smiled back and went to find Soumaya. When I found her she was talking with some guy. I watched as she perfectly dismissed the guy. There was something about the freedom Soumaya always had that I envied. Everyone around us was dancing, if you could call it that, all over each other. They were basically having sex on the dance floor like wild animals.

"Are you alright?" she asked.

"Yeah, that guy just came up to me and said, 'We meet again', it was so weird. I've never met him before. Did he look familiar to you?"

She looked over toward where I had come from. We were probably thinking the same thing. That it's happened to us before. Someone met one of us and then thought we were the other one when they saw us again. It happens with identical twins. Now the only difference was the hairstyle. She kept her hair more natural. In my world, I wanted my hair straight.

Do you remember that one episode of *Sister Sister* when Tia and Tamera went from their pre-teen curly hair to straight hair? That was us. But Soumaya hadn't caved to the pressure and got the same style as me. She's always been able to have her own mind. I think that's why I admire her so much.

She looked over at the guy one last time but shook her head. "No. I don't think so. Maybe it was just a pickup line," she teased.

"I don't think so. But it doesn't matter. The bartender told me the teams are upstairs and they're good. I think I might just stay back and see what they do tonight."

"I mean if you really want to," she said, checking her phone. "We only have to stay until midnight and then we can go home, put pajamas on, and eat ice cream while we binge murder mysteries until we fall asleep."

"Now that sounds good," I said, putting my arm with her as we grabbed our drinks and went out to the floor to dance with each other.

An hour later, we were sweaty and tired as the countdown began. The crowd started getting excited. Sixty seconds to go. This huge guy, had to be at least six and a half feet, dark chocolate skin, brown eyes, and a jawline that could slice through metal. We'd been eyeing each other for the last five minutes.

"Go get him," she said into my ear.

I started to move toward him. Soumaya smacked me on my ass and sent me on my way. We came together shyly, both of us timid but ready for a New Year's Kiss. No words were exchanged. Only a knowing smile.

"TEN!" everyone called out.

"NINE!"

His fingertips traced up my arm giving me goosebumps all over my body. It was like electricity bathing me in energy. I was going to kiss him in less than ten seconds.

"EIGHT!"

"SEVEN!"

I was readying myself. I knew it was going to be a kiss that could change everything.

"SIX!"

"FIVE, FOUR, THREE..."

He came closer.

"TWO!"

His lips were almost on mine. I could feel the anticipation of midnight coming.

"ONE!"

His lips pressed on mine were everything. He pulled me close, one hand splaying over my back, and the other coming to gently caress my neck. Want and need heated my core. I needed to walk away from him so that I could keep an eye on the players in the VIP room above us.

I steadily pulled away. My lips felt the absence of his warmth. With the slightest sway I regained my balance by placing my hand on his hard, muscular chest.

I turned around looking for Soumaya. She was gone. I looked around the entire dance floor of couples celebrating the new year.

He chuckled. "You're not already looking for someone else, are you?"

"No, but I've got to find my sister," I said as I reached out to shake his hand.

He gathered my hand in his and pressed my hand in between both of his. He engulfed my hand entirely with his warmth. I looked up into his dark brown eyes. There was something in his eyes about how I offered my hand. He was amused by me.

I turned to go find Soumaya, but he caught me by my arm. "Can I get your name?"

"It's Zee."

"Zee? That's all? Like Madonna?"

"Exactly," I said, giving him a teasing smile and then walking off.

I walked into the bathroom expecting that she would be inside. It was the only place left she could have gone. "Where are you, Sou?" I asked myself as I looked around in the ladies bathroom for her.

"Who you lookin' for, Sweetheart?" a woman asked me who was reapplying her lipstick in the mirror at the sink.

"My sister. She looks like me."

"Like she's wearing the same thing?" she asked, sounding stupid.

"No, we're twins. She's got curly hair, though."

"Nope, haven't seen another you," she said, finishing up with her lipstick and putting it into her Hermès purse.

There was no way I'd miss that band. Classic and expensive. She saw me eyeing her purse and smirked as she walked past me. *Judgy bitch.* I looked around the crowded ladies room one more time, but she wasn't there. I walked back out to the floor and started my way around the people celebrating everywhere. I was getting bumped from every direction. I was done.

5

LUTHER 'ZEUS' ZEUSES

*L*ast night I had an amazing kiss with a girl I actually was interested in seeing again, and I let her go. This girl made my toes curl. I stretched out in bed starfish style, rolling my ankles, and warming up my muscles. I looked over at my phone, wirelessly charging on the Bluetooth dock, and noticed the screen light up.

Picking up my phone, I checked to see what notifications were going off. The first wasn't so bad. It was the same ole thing with the paparazzi. Photos of Dom and me in front of Double Down last night. That I was used to. It was the story attached to the photos of us where Dom was wearing the exact same thing that he was wearing last night while he was fucking a woman. Even though the photo wasn't super clear, I'd recognize the girl I kissed at midnight anywhere.

"What the fuck?" I growled in my empty room.

I went over the online story a hundred times before I threw my phone across the room and pulled on workout clothes so that I could go to my gym and work off the anger I had.

I pulled into the parking lot at Olympic Gym. I had opened my own gym after so many athletes were being treated like goldfish as the other gym members came to gawk at us. I put my own money into my own gym, and now I've got six locations all over the country. Professional athletes have praised how comfortable the workout environment is. No one stands around and gawks. There's support, but nobody is there to take photos or try to get autographs.

I nodded to my staff as I walked through the door. I made sure to have enough staff to handle the New Year Resolution season. It seemed like the first three months of the year we'd get at least a thirty percent increase before it started dying down and the people who set all these goals realize that gym life isn't for everyone. It's fine if you find your own way to be healthy and workout. It doesn't have to be in the gym.

I made my way into my office to store my things and then went out to get some reps in before I go out to one of the trails for a run.

Halfway through my reps, I received a notification. My earbuds read off the text message.

"You have a new message from Dom D'Angelo: Where are you? I need your advice."

I didn't respond. I wasn't ready to talk to him. Seeing even a blurry photo made me so angry. Why can he do whatever he wants and get away with it? Well, not this time. It was splashed all over. In the top trending searched stories. Everyone was trying to pick up an update on who the woman in the photo was.

The more I sweated, the better I felt. I came to the understanding that my best friend hadn't known that I was interested in her. It was her that kissed me and then went off to fuck him without any regard for anyone else. It was her that my anger landed on in the end, and I wasn't going to let my best friend get drug through the dirt for someone who could kiss someone so passionately and then run off to fuck someone else the next.

After my run, I went into the showers. Every shower stall was private, and there wasn't anyone inside. I hopped into the steamy shower to clean up. Ten minutes later, I was in a towel drying off and then getting dressed for the rest of the day.

I went into my office and pulled out my phone. I saw the fifteen missed calls from Dom and all the text messages. I tapped his name on the missed calls so my phone could start dialing. It was barely two rings in when he answered.

"Where the fuck have you been? I needed you," he said, sounding pissed off and anxious.

"Sorry man, I was getting in a workout. I saw social media this morning," I explained.

I wouldn't hide anything from him. I learned at an early age that secrets within a team made for bad playing on the field.

"That's exactly why I'm calling. Coach has me scheduled to come in for a conference with the new PR Manager later."

"I heard we were getting a new PR Manager. What do you think he's going to say?"

"He's a she. Some woman named Zeri Williams. Conway is completely smitten with her," Dom said.

I hadn't heard anything about the new PR Manager being a female. That should be interesting with the whole lot of us players. We can be pretty obnoxious. I've been with the Scavengers for a long time, and none of us are choir boys.

"Interesting." I chuckled. "I wish her luck. She's going to need it with the fuck up you've gotten yourself into."

"That's why I need your help. I don't want to leave this in the hands of someone who doesn't know me, doesn't know what happened, and doesn't even care about the girl. She's the one who got her body blasted all over the internet."

Was that Dom's heart on display? He's never acted like this before over anyone. Well, maybe his half-sister Makenna and his niece Emmalynn. It's surprising how that bastard ending up with a baby that cute—had to be all Makenna's genetics. He would have never let any of us even look at her, but Mason Cooper came in on his gallant steed and whisked her off her feet.

"You actually like this girl?" I asked.

After a long pause, he finally spoke. "Yeah, man, I think I do. This wasn't the first time I've run into her. I've been trying to find her."

"Is she your Retriever girl you've been obsessed over?"

"Yeah." He chuckled. "I've got to see her again."

I wasn't with her first. Dom was. Now my problem wasn't that she was with me first; it was that she was with me at all if she was with Dom. She was playing both of us. I couldn't let this woman make a fool of my best friend. As public figures, we're constantly dealing with fame seekers or gold diggers. Had one woman take a fan picture with me, and the next thing I know, she's got that I slept with her and she was pregnant with my baby all over social media.

He was still going on about how amazing she was when my thoughts came back to the conversation.

"... there's something about her. I'm completely drawn to her, and she's different."

"Dom, man," I sighed, "I—"

"You're right. I should figure out if I can get this Zeri Williams to help me get in contact with her. Thanks, man. I've got to go. Drayden is calling me."

That fucker hung up on me. I pulled my phone away from my ear and stared at the screen. "Fine, I will go to you," I said as I brought up my text messages with Dom and sent him a message.

Zeus: When's your meeting?

I waited and waited without response. I would have to act fast. I grabbed my keys and called our coach.

"Zeus, what can I do for you? Today was supposed to be a rest day," he said, answering his phone.

"I know, Coach. I wanted to know when Dom was meeting with you today," I asked.

"Are you involved in this shit?" Coach spat.

"No... yes... maybe. I don't fucking know."

"Whoa, whoa, whoa, I'm going to need more information here."

I didn't want to tell Coach what was going on. He wouldn't ever let it go. He's been on all of us single guys to stop doing stupid shit. That's probably why this Williams woman got hired. I bet she's some fifty-year-old hardass who chain smokes and thinks that all men are manwhores.

"I need to talk to Dom first. It's not right he doesn't know since it involves him," I said.

I heard a grumbling through the line. Something, as one of his players, I was fairly used to. We're all idiots and are the constant bane of his existence. At least that's what he says.

"I can't say that I understand, but as long as you're not doing anything stupid, I'm fine with it," Coach said. "We're meeting in the conference room later with Bill Conway."

Oh shit, it's already gotten to the owner. I wasn't looking to sit down with Bill Conway, but I needed to see Dom before he did something stupid.

"What time?"

"Are you planning on attending?" Coach asked just as I heard a loud noise. "Get off your brother!"

I silently chuckled. Coach Hobbs and his wife, April, had six kids. One right after another. The oldest was eighteen, or something like that, and I'm pretty sure the youngest age was still being counted in months. They were the real stressors in Coach's life. But he wanted his boy, and he finally got one.

"KNOCK IT THE FUCK OUT! You're worse than my players," he yelled then finished grumbling into the phone. "I've got to go."

"Yeah, of course," I said, but he had already hung up.

I laughed wanting that kind of life for myself one day. The picnics April hosts in the spring every year are fantastic. And she always makes at least five different kinds of desserts, including at least one cheesecake. It's delicious. I always sneak an extra slice, and then one of Coach's kids tattles on me.

I needed to get home and get changed so that I could make it to the conference with Dom. I had to tell him everything before he did something stupid.

Grabbing my keys from my desk drawer, I walked toward the front reception desk.

"You leaving for the day?" Denis asked.

"I might be back. I know today could get busier," I said, looking at my watch. "I've got a meeting, and depending on how it goes, I might not be able to get back."

"Okay, I think we will be fine. It might be a good thing for you to be MIA when new clients come in. Especially the women. They don't need to know that you are here all the time when you're not in practice," he said with a chuckle.

I let out a raspy laugh.

We've had tons of women come in because they've heard that professional athletes workout here. When they don't actually do any working out, they get a strike against them. After three strikes, they're out. Literally. They get put on the list and are banned from coming into the gym.

"As long as it's not Linda again," I replied, knowing that everyone knew about Linda. She was like the *Karen* of the gym.

"I will catapult myself over this counter to lock that door if I see her red Fiat pull into the parking lot."

I barked out a laugh imagining Denis doing this. He hated her. She kept complaining about the athletes using the machines so that she couldn't use any of them. She was the one who always wanted to use the machines that were being used by other people. Then she would start yelling at the person using the machine. One of us would come intervene to help, but she was never happy. I finally had to talk to her about her behavior and how it was distracting and creating a negative workout environment for everyone else. Linda spent the next forty-five minutes yelling obscenities at me and cursing my future children before she tried to slap me the way Will Smith smacked Chris Rock—completely unprovoked and unnecessary. Before anyone comes for me, we all know Will Smith thought it was funny before he looked at Jada's face. And who really cares? That moment, that joke would have never been remembered, and it became the only memorable, talked about moment from that awards show. I would have turned around and sued the hell out of Will Smith. Chris Rock is now at the top of my list of my favorite black celebrities.

"Oh God, yeah, I can't deal with anymore Lindas," I said.

"That's why we screen everyone."

"That's right. I'll see you later," I said as I waved and walked out of the front door.

On my drive home, I started trying to figure out what I was going to say to Dom. How do you even explain something like that? *Hey, Dom, the girl you're so excited about basically had her tongue down my throat just a few minutes before you had your dick inside of her.* Yeah, that sounds like I will get punched in the face. Again, circling back to Will Smith.

I put on the required *game day* uniform to go in to see the owner of the Scavengers, Bill Conway. One of his pet peeves was for us to always be in *game day* uniform when meeting anyone outside the rink or in a professional situation. It didn't have to be a suit, but it must look sharp. Athletic pants are a no go. In fact, a memo came down telling us not to be caught in the gray sweatpants trend. No dong imprints allowed on social media.

Charcoal dress pants and a burgundy sweater with a white shirt underneath that peeked out right at the collar. I grabbed my leather jacket and square toed dress shoes to finish out my outfit and get to the conference so I can tell Dom everything.

I practiced what I was going to say to him over and over on the way there. None of it sounded good.

I pulled into the lot and found a spot close to the door. As soon as I got out and locked my SUV, I started going over my words again.

"I don't know how to tell you this, but the woman you were

with was kissing me just before she agreed to go off with you," I said to myself, walking into the building. "She's playing you," I continued, rubbing my fingers on my temples as I pressed the elevator's up button.

"Who's playing who?" I heard Dom from behind me.

The ding of the elevator's doors opening gave me an extra thirty seconds to try to figure out how to start.

He chuckled. "You look like you just got called into the owner's office and your head is on the chopping block."

I licked my lips trying to get out what I needed to say. We stepped onto the elevator to go up to the conference room, and Dom pressed the number three on the elevator panel.

He looked over at me and said, "Are you meeting with someone?"

I cleared my throat and coughed into my hand. "I... uh, I'm here for you."

"Well, thanks, man, I appreciate it. I'm not really sure what they're going to tell me to do."

I opened my mouth to rip off the Band-Aid and tell him everything, but he started speaking before I could say anything.

"I really want to get her number. Even a fucking name at this point would be more than what I got," he said, tapping my shoulder. "She's beautiful, funny, and I've got to see her again."

His demeanor had completely changed. He was acting like he had when he got a puppy for his eighth birthday. He loved that dog. He's never gotten over Rex's death.

I sighed, "Dom, I've got to tell you something."

My tone alone made his face drop and concern appear. I hated doing this, but here we go.

"Go ahead," he said.

"The girl from the photo..." I started, looking straight into his eyes. "I kissed her. She kissed me."

"What?" he asked, sounding confused.

"Yeah, man, I didn't want to tell you, but we kissed," I explained quickly and then just waited.

It looked as though he was processing every possible emotion from the information about the girl he was enamored with. He pressed his fingers into his brow and rubbed.

"Okay, wait, when did you kiss her?" he asked, his voice slightly deeper than normal.

"Last night," I admitted.

"What the fuck?" he snapped.

"Yeah, we'd both been looking at each other, and when midnight hit, I made my way to her."

He looked at me confused. "That's not possible."

"Yeah, it is. I kissed her."

"No, I mean I kissed her at midnight and then took her up to Nix's office."

This time, I was the one that was confused.

"No, I swear I kissed her at midnight. Then she basically ran from me looking for her... sister. Fuck me. She probably has a sister that looks like her, and you were with that one."

"That's got to be it. There's no other way we could have kissed the same girl at midnight," he said, then just as the elevator doors opened, he tapped the back of his hand on my stomach and said, "I'm guessing I'm the only one who got laid though." A chuckle came out as he walked off the elevator and started walking toward the conference room.

"Well, fuck you too," I said under my breath.

He barked out a laugh, which made everyone look over at us.

6

ZERI WILLIAMS

That morning I answered my phone to hear Bill Conway, owner of the Scavengers, booming his outrage over the newest fuck up from one of his players. Unfortunately, I already knew what this one was about.

"Ms. Williams, what are you going to do about this scandal?" Bill Conway's voice was gruff and stern.

I was about to get a scolding that I didn't deserve.

"Weren't you there with them last night? All the tabloids are saying the photo was from last night. You can nearly see her nipples. What are you going to do about this?" Bill went on and on.

"Bill, I promise you this was completely unknown. Not only had I not met up with any of the team to even introduce myself, but D'Angelo had been in the VIP section most of the night. I didn't have access to their party. Something you failed to tell me."

"Are you insinuating that I set you up to fail? Weren't you the one that persuaded an entire building worth of people to let you into my office?" he asked, giving me the opportunity to realize the blame wasn't on either of us.

"I'm sorry, sir. I will speak with the woman from the photo and be prepared with a statement shortly."

"Good. There will be a conference call later with everyone. Be on it. I'll have Janet send you the information."

I'd spent the entire day with my stomach in knots and trying to get to the bottom of who could have done this. Once we spoke with Phoenix Drayden, I at least felt more confident about the fact that whoever this asshole was, he wouldn't be able to put more private images up.

After we went to Double Down and spoke with Drayden, Soumaya ended up picking up a call from Retriever that took our day in a different direction. I'd end up speaking with their legal department because the human resource department wanted to have Soumaya come in on her day off, not on the clock, to sign something releasing her from her position. I think not.

And, of course, all this would take place within the next hour.

"Zeri, you there?" Jared Hobbs' deep voice came through the speaker on my phone.

Jared Hobbs was a good man. Coach for the Scavengers and he's put up with his players' crap for years. I was there to help him get these guys under control. We've had a few conversations where he's talked about his troublemakers. Neither Dominic D'Angelo or Zeus Zeuses were on that list.

"I'm here, Jared," I replied, looking at Soumaya.

She looked worried. I'd of course handle yet another of her fuck ups. Perhaps remind her of this moment for the next month.

"Great, I want to make this as clear as possible; we don't want a scandal," he said.

"Understood. I've talked with the other party and come up with the best possible press release. I'm emailing that to you now," I said as I picked up my tablet and swiped on the screen to get into my email. "If you all will read over the statement, we can make any changes necessary, but this is the best possible way to move forward."

"What makes you think there won't be more leaked images or even a tape?" Another man I hadn't recognized the gruff voice for asked.

"Well, I can state that, as of right now, I've contacted the owner of the club and have gotten a name from the credit card that was used. I have already taken the liberty to get documentation for arrest," I explained.

"How'd you get that?" Another deep voice came over the line.

"It's my job," I replied. I felt insulted that I had to defend myself against the idea that I didn't do my due diligence to prepare for this meeting. The moment that I had spoken with Bill Conway, I knew I'd have to bring my A game and make sure that none of the stank from the scandal touched Soumaya.

"No, I mean I had just talked with Nix. He didn't even have that," he snapped back.

"Again, this is my job. I realize I can't make this just go away, but I can minimize the fallout. Especially for the other party, since she was the one to be photographed topless."

The line was quiet for a long time. I was getting worried, but I couldn't show my sister that I was worried. These men could take over the conversation at any point, and I would never get another word in.

"Do we need to address the girl in the image?" Conway asked.

"How do you mean?" I asked.

"Is she going to come at D'Angelo for money?" he replied as if that was the most normal thing to say.

"Absolutely not!" Soumaya snapped before I could stop her.

There were two things I absolutely despised: people confusing Soumaya and me and calling either one of our intentions or morals into question.

"Wait, who was that?" Dominic asked. "Is that her?" He

must have pounded on a table, which boomed through the speaker.

I just looked at Soumaya like 'yeah, you fucked up. I told you not to say anything' and then took a deep breath. "I am with the other party from the image."

"What's your name?" he asked. I stood there looking at Soumaya, waiting for her to decide what she was going to do. She could either tell him the truth and be sucked into his world or tell them that she didn't want that. I saw the moment she decided. She liked him.

"Soumaya," she replied.

"Soumaya," he said with a longing sigh. "I want to see you again."

My face hardened. My eyes went wide, and I clenched my jaw together. Having Soumaya and Dominic D'Angelo be seen together after they had a private photo leaked could end so badly. I shook my head—the slightest no but making sure she knew it was a warning.

"No," she said meekly.

"Why not?" He went on as though it would have been impossible for anyone to turn him down. "Do you have a boyfriend?"

"Well, no."

"That's good. Meet me for dinner tonight," he rushed to get out.

"I can't," she said apologetically as she looked straight at me.

"I don't think it would be a good idea for them to be seen in public with the photograph just hitting the media," I explained to fill the silence.

"Hmm, actually, I think it might be just what D'Angelo needs," Jared offered.

"I don't know," I said. "It could go really bad. Perhaps we can talk privately before any decisions are made. There's an outside situation happening that could be affected by a continued relationship with Mr. D'Angelo."

"What outside situation?" he demanded.

"Soumaya's current position with her employer is in danger with this photograph and story hitting most media outlets," I explained for her.

"At Retriever?" he asked.

I looked over at her and mouthed, "How'd he know?"

"She'd rather not say at this time. She would like to keep as much of her privacy at this time," I replied for her.

"Come on, I need something. I can't just walk away from this. I know how I felt when I saw you last night. I'm not ready to walk away..." The long pregnant pause nearly killed both of us. "I think you should date me. Give the fans something to root for. Coach is right. It'll go away."

7

LUTHER 'ZEUS' ZEUSES

That conference call was going nowhere. My buddy was like a sinking ship with no captain. He wasn't getting anything. We all waited as patiently as possible to hear this girl's final decision.

I looked over at Dom. He was sitting on the edge of his chair, his hands gripping the edge of the table, and he was staring at the triangular conference speaker you see in movies as if it was about to either give him the world or reject him from society.

"Come on, Soumaya, I know there's something there between us. Give it a chance," Dom said.

"Okay."

We all heard the uncertainty in her voice.

Dom looked over at me. He had the biggest smile on his face. I was happy for my best friend. Now was my opportunity.

"Soumaya, do you have a sister?" I asked.

Silence. Pure and utter silence.

"Hello?" I asked to see if she had hung up.

"Um... yeah, I have a sister," Soumaya replied.

"Can I get her number? I think I met her last night, and I wanted to see her again."

Silence.

"What's going on here?" Coach asked.

"I just wanted to see if she wanted to go out on a date. She disappeared. I looked for her, but I couldn't find her."

"He looked for you?" Soumaya whispered.

"Wait, is she there?" I questioned.

"I'm sorry we're going to have to end this early. I've got to get Soumaya on with her employer. Everyone have a great rest of your day, and I'll email the changes to the statement right over to you, Bill."

"Okay, thanks," Bill Conway said as the line clicked and went dead.

"That was weird," Coach said.

"It was," Dom agreed.

"Is this something else that's going to pop up that you fucked her in this club?" Conway snapped.

"No, it was a kiss at midnight. She walked away before I could even get her name," I explained.

Conway's eyebrow quirked in question.

"It looks like she doesn't want to talk to me anyways," I said, standing from the chair.

"Zeus–" Dom started.

"Don't worry about it," I said, shaking my head.

"No, I'll ask Soumaya about her. I'm sure once I have her alone, she'll tell me," Dom said, standing and patting me on my shoulder.

"I'm not done with the two of you." Bill Conway snapped his fingers and then pointed at the chairs for us to sit back down.

"You thought we'd get out of this a lot easier, didn't you?" I asked Dom.

He tapped his pointer finger on his nose twice and smiled.

We looked over at Coach, but he shrugged and took his phone out of his jacket pocket. He hadn't seemed worried about what Mr. Conway was going to say or do, so I tried to relax. I still wasn't the one that got caught with their pants down and cock out. Not to say that it couldn't have been. If my girl would have let me take her into the back, then I would have taken the same opportunity that Dom had with his lady.

"He's mad, right?" I asked.

"Oh, yeah," he mouthed and then looked back to Mr. Conway to start.

It was nearly an entire minute before he even looked over at either of us. The look that Dom gave me clearly indicated him asking if we should take bets on what he was going to say.

We have been friends long enough for both of us to be able to give each other looks and know exactly what the other was thinking.

"You two are going to be the death of me. It seems like every time something happens, the two of you are at the center of it. Why is that?" Conway said as he crossed his arms over his chest.

I looked over to Dom for a response.

"I don't know what to say," Dom said.

"And what about you?" Conway asked, looking directly at me.

I opened and closed my mouth like a fish trying to figure out what he wanted to hear from us.

We haven't been choir boys, not in the slightest, but we aren't that bad. I mean we are the reason last season that our opponents did end up Smurf'd after a game. They had to get back on their bus dyed Smurf blue, and then they were blue for their next three games. The team's social media account happened to put a comparison picture between the actual Smurfs and a photo of them that had gone viral over social media with the statement 'Don't be blue just because you lost to us.' It hit over nine million likes, and we have no idea how any of it happened.

"Well, the two of you better figure it out," Conway said, standing from the chair at the head of the table and starting to pace back and forth then said, "There better not be another Smurf incident."

I sincerely tried, but I couldn't hold back the laugh. I couldn't keep it in any longer.

"Stop it," Coach snapped.

Of course that only made Dom and I both start laughing. After a moment of us unable to stop laughing, Mr. Conway and Coach Hobbs finally joined in.

"That was pretty funny. The Gladiators will never live it down," Coach offered.

That made Mr. Conway laugh harder.

Perhaps he'd forget about everything that made him pissed off at us in the first place.

When the laughter died down, Mr. Conway looked over at us and very sternly said, "That can't happen again. There will be no pranks, jokes, or any kind of hijinks or shenanigans. Do you understand me?"

"Yes, sir," Dom and I said together with our heads lowered like scolded dogs.

"Good, get the hell out of here," he said.

"Um... when can I get Soumaya's information?" Dom asked.

"I'll get Ms. Williams to send over her contact information to get this plan put into action. Just don't fuck it up," Coach Hobbs replied as he escorted us out of the conference room.

"That went pretty well," Dom said with the biggest smile on his face.

"What makes you think that?" I asked.

"Because I'm going to get to see her again, and I'm going to get her to 'fake' date me long enough so that she actually wants to date me," he explained as we walked toward the elevators with Coach.

"Do you really want to date this girl? It's not just wanting to get your dick wet?" I asked.

He narrowed his eyes on me. "If you want me to get her sister's information, you better be nice to her. I know you already don't like her. What's that about? Is it because you thought she was trying to play both of us?"

"No," I snapped. "I just think if she was so willing to sneak off and fuck you in a public place that she cared more about what you can do for her and not you."

"Aww, Zeus, do you really care that much about me? I'm touched," he said, putting his hand over his heart and acting as if he really cared.

"Fuck you," I snapped as the elevator door opened and I walked off, hoping to get away from his over-acting portrayal of how much he cared about me.

"Where are you going?" Dom asked.

"I've got to get back to the gym. It's resolution season."

He barked out a laugh. We all knew exactly what resolution season meant. I doubted I'd get anywhere with the sister in the next week. I needed to just focus on the gym and the team.

"See ya later, man," I said, slapping hands with him.

"Yeah, if I get to talk to Soumaya today, I'll let you know about her sister."

"Thanks, man, but I doubt it's going to happen after the way they hung up with us."

"No kidding," he murmured as he walked off.

Once I got into my truck, I automatically drove back to my gym and parked at the back of the lot so that the new customers could come in and sign up without thinking we are so busy they'd never get to use any of the equipment. It had only started being a problem. I'd have to get some more high end equipment for those who wanted a traditional gym and some more equipment for the *heathens* as I like to call them. Don't worry, I'm a heathen. I'd rather be out on the blacktop with a heavy weight tire than picking up weights. My new favorite gym buddy, Ryan, comes in and lifts the four and five hundred pound tires, and we've talked about getting a couple of six hundred pound ones.

I walked back through the front door to see Denis with a

couple that was asking questions about the gym. I gave him a head nod and walked past him.

"Was that..." the man asked.

"Yes. Luther Zeuses is the proud owner of Olympic Gym," Denis responds.

"Who's Luther Zeuses?" the woman asked.

"He's a linebacker for the Scavengers," the man explained.

"So he plays football."

I chuckled under my breath.

Her husband scoffed at her. "He's not just a linebacker. He's *the* best linebacker in the league."

That's one hell of a compliment. I wouldn't say I was the best, but I'm not going to tell the man to change his opinion.

"I appreciate the compliment," I said, putting my hand out to shake his.

He nervously put his hand into mine to shake my hand. I shook his wife's hand afterward, giving her a smile, and then asked, "Are you thinking about becoming members?"

"We are."

"Well, let me recommend attending any of our classes. Not only are our members supportive, but the classes are divided by gender for less distraction and optimal progress," I explained.

"Well, we were wanting to work out together," the wife replied.

"You can, but I will offer that I have seen couples come in and do fantastic working out together, but they also really enjoy and stay with us when they develop other workout support systems. I think if you manage time together and time apart, you will get more out of your workout. You may want a different workout than your husband, and he may focus more on building muscle one day, while you're looking for strength training or low-impact cardio. Those would be good days to see if there's a spot open for a class or join a friend on the floor. I'm sure Denis would be happy to take you on a tour around the floor and talk with you about what can be available to you."

The wife was smiling and nodding as I spoke. I got her right where I wanted her.

"I'll see you guys in a little bit," I said as Denis moved to take them around the floor and walk them outside to the trails and the *Wild Man* section, which has the tires and other larger equipment.

I checked the desk to see Jill come over and take over while Denis was on the tour.

"Hey Zeus, how are you?" Jill asked.

At one point I would have been happy with her attention. We may have had something a couple years ago, but not anymore. She's been seeing someone, and I haven't really felt the need to hide from her for a while.

"Good. How are you?" I asked, feeling awkward for the first time in months around her.

"Good, I guess. Roger and I decided to call it quits."

Ah, fuck my life. That's why it felt awkward. Was she gearing up to flirt with me? I gotta shut that shit down.

"Sorry to hear that. I'm sure there is someone better out there for you," I said, regretting it immediately.

"I hope so," she said, looking me up and down.

"You will, just like I did," I lied.

Her face changed drastically. "I didn't know you were seeing anyone."

"Yeah, I met her through Dom. His girlfriend's sister," I explained, giving her enough information for her to stop and not enough for her to think I might have been making it all up.

"Was that the girl from the photo that's all over the tabloids? Didn't he just meet her?" she asked, snippily.

A low grumble came from the back of my throat in frustration. "That's inappropriate of you to discuss."

She looked at me meekly and said, "I'm sorry. I didn't really mean anything by it."

"Just don't let it happen again," I said, confirming what she said was not okay.

She nodded in agreement, and I walked away to go to my office to make sure that payroll was executed and that the schedule for next pay period was completed and posted. After Jill came at me, all I felt like doing was going out to the *Wild Man* area and throwing around some weight.

I went to get changed into some athletic sweats. I'd work out until my anger was gone and I wouldn't just fire her. I was close when she started talking about Dom and his girl.

I've never seen Dom the way he was when he talked to Soumaya over the phone. The only other time his eyes lit up the way they had was when he found out he was going to be an uncle. Emmalynn is not only a mascot for the Badgers, but she spends some time on the field with the Scavengers too.

I spent about an hour and a half sweating and making myself feel better. It's nothing like a practice with my team, but it got the anger out of me. The only thing that was still weighing on me was the girl that didn't want to even tell me her name.

8

ZERI WILLIAMS

I was happy when the phone call with Retriever turned out in Soumaya's favor. She had been so worried she was going to lose her job with Retriever. I knew how much she loved working for them. Her clients were amazing, and she was constantly receiving more client requests.

I wasn't going to let her fuckwad of a manager tear her down and then lie to get her fired. I requested Soumaya's personnel file from Retriever's corporate office. Once they emailed me the file, I poured over it. I found several compliments that coincided with strict write-ups and disciplines.

I knew I had them going into the phone call—as long as I'd have an opportunity to speak. And even though I did speak, I could tell Mr. Worstmount wanted to speak over me. He didn't want to be found out that he created all these problems.

The best part was that the photograph of Soumaya and Dominic never even got brought up. The focus was completely on the disillusions from Mr. Worstmount.

It was when Soumaya started asking why I didn't give Zeus my number. I wanted to... I just couldn't. I'd eventually have to talk to him and explain. As good as I was at my job and coming up with the perfect thing to say, I had zero clues what to say to fix my situation.

"What should I do about Dom?" Soumaya asked, bringing me out of my own mind.

"I'm going to pass your information along, and from the way he reacted, I'm going to say you should be prepared for him to call," I said.

She started to pick at her cuticle around her thumbnail.

"Stop that. He obviously likes you. He even wanted to see you again after you gave away the milk for free."

She snorted. "Thanks, Mom."

"Speaking of... after you see him again, you're going to need to talk to him about meeting Mom and Dad," I reminded her.

She put her hands over her eyes and shook her head back and forth. "Why?" she whined.

"Because you slept with a professional football player in a fairly public place."

She winced. "Have you heard anything about the guy who sold the photo?"

I sighed. "Not yet. But I have high hopes. At this point, no media outlet will be publishing any more elicit photos without permission. Someone will give him up, and then we can have him arrested."

"I really want him arrested."

"I know. But in the meantime, keep focusing on what we need to do, and I guess, *date* Dominic D'Angelo."

After a long pause, she finally spoke. "What do you know about him?"

"Not a lot. I haven't gotten to his file."

She shot up straight and asked, "You have his file?"

"Well, yeah, but I think it will be better if you get to know him for him and not what's in the file. You never know, there could be something real there."

She snorted. "Zee, I'm going to let you in on a big TMI. He

fucked me like a wild animal. There's no way he wants to find the girl next door and bring her home to meet his mother."

"Oh," I said, holding my hands up and waving my hands so she wouldn't go on, "I didn't need to know that."

On some level, we've always known each other's preferences and proclivities. Soumaya has always had a more submissive attitude with her partners. For her to tell me that he was dominant with her told me how much she truly enjoyed it. I prefer an even dominant/submissive relationship. I love to be in control. And I love to find the compromise to get everyone something they want. Relationships should be a compromise. You should enjoy being with the person in your relationship.

"I know. But you might as well. If that asshole took the video, then you'll probably get to see a whole lot more of it than you wanted to," she joked, but it really wasn't funny.

"Sou, it's going to be alright. I swear," I said, giving her a hug. "I'm going to go write up the statement and then send it off to Bill so he can see it and approve it for the media. They're going to want to get photos of the *happy couple* out on a date or two."

I pinched my lower lip between my thumb and pointer finger, thinking. I could get the two of them out doing some volunteer work and really up their image as a couple.

"Sou? How do you feel about doing something with D'Angelo that can be shown off as some volunteer work?"

She had peeked over her railing to look at me while I talked to her.

"Like what?" she asked.

"Maybe some time at an animal shelter or doing something at a primary school."

She thought for a moment. "Yeah, I could do that. I like kids and dogs."

"Good, I'll mention that when I email your number. Be prepared. I think he's going to call you the minute he's got your number in his hand."

She nodded as she pulled her head back from over the railing. I knew she was nervous; however, I knew she'd be able to handle it.

She was probably listening to music with her headphones on, laying on her bed, looking up at the ceiling. She's always done that when she needed to chill out and get her anxiety under control.

As soon as I get to my computer, I make the changes Bill asked me to make and then attach Soumaya's cell phone number. As soon as I pressed send, I dialed Bill's number.

"Zeri? What in hell was that?" he answered.

"I'm so sorry about that. There was some confusion, and the call ended because of it." I tried to explain without explaining everything.

A sigh of frustration came through the line. "I've got to tell you I'm not impressed with the fact you made this girl..." papers rustled and then he continued, "Soumaya and her sister are a priority over the team you were actually hired to protect."

"I understand. I am very sorry about that. After talking with Ms.--" I paused, realizing I was about to use our last name and quickly picked back up, "Soumaya, I realized she needed someone on her side. Without giving you too much information, last night was the first time she'd ever done anything like that and had regrets. You know what could happen when a female decides she regrets a one night stand."

He sighed. "I agree. It was good that she was comforted. I don't know what would have happened had Ron been in charge of this situation."

Ron Reihmer was the old PR manager. He suuuuuucked at his job. The last thing anyone would have wanted was for Ron to release any statement. He gave horrible advice, and now two of our players not only have arrest records, but they are doing community service for the next year. Before you think they did something horrible, no, they stopped on the interstate to help in an accident, and they caused a pileup. Stupid, right? It should have been all about the fact that they stopped to help, but of course not. By the time they got ahold of Ron, they were already arrested and stayed in jail over the weekend. Ron was cheating on his wife in a Motel 6 with a pay-by-the-hour hooker. He *was* his own PR scandal.

"I promise you everything that has been said is on behalf of the team and keeping this less than desirable situation from becoming a nightmare," I said, hoping he would believe that I wasn't trying to hide anything.

He sighed.

Again with the sighing. I guess that would be his tell when he came to terms with something out of his control.

"I just sent over the new statement."

"Okay," he said then went quiet.

"Bill?"

"I'm reading," he said.

"Okay. Sorry."

After a long pause, he finally spoke.

"Yeah, that sounds good. Do we need to do a background check on this girl?"

"I've already taken the liberty. She's a catch."

A relieved sigh came through the line. "Good."

"I've even talked with her about doing some sort of volunteer date out in public," I added.

I could imagine Bill lighting up with excitement. Getting the players involved in more volunteer work was part of the deal. He wanted to see them out at charity events and helping kids. I promised I knew what I was doing and that it was going to be worth it all.

I already had the team set to come to practice for the junior league in the next month, a photo op at a park cleanup, and my personal favorite—reading with a kindergarten class at one of the low income schools in the city.

"Yes, I like that," he replied distractedly. "Do you think it would be too much to tip off the tabloids…"

"I may make sure that they go somewhere where there might already be coverage."

"That's why I hired you. It's like you're inside my head. So, you've got this?" he asked.

"Yes, sir. I've got this," I said, feeling the most uneasy I've ever felt answering a question.

"Good, I don't want any more surprises."

"No surprises, got it," I replied.

I heard his assistant in the background speaking to him. "Okay, yeah, tell him I'll just be one more minute," he said, speaking away from the receiver. "Alright, Zeri, don't let me down."

Before I could say anything else, he hung up. I shook my head. He was direct. I'm pretty sure I will eventually hear him say something like, "Time is money."

In the distance, there's a ping. It's either Mom or... D'Angelo.

"ZEE!"

It's D'Angelo.

Soumaya came running downstairs, nearly tripping at the bottom of the stairs.

"He wants to talk to me," she said, her eyes nearly bugging out of her head and her anxiety rising right before my eyes.

"What did he say?" I asked.

She handed me her phone and squeezed in close to me at the table.

Unknown Number: Hey, this is Dom. Can I call you now?

"Can he?" I asked.

"I don't know. I guess I wasn't prepared for him to call me."

I took the liberty and texted him back for her.

Me: Yes.

Her phone started ringing almost immediately.

"Talk to him," I said, handing back her phone. "Answer it."

She touched the screen and then put it up to her ear. A deep voice came through inaudibly for me, but she smiled.

9

LUTHER 'ZEUS' ZEUSES

I tossed and turned the entire night. Memories of my father leaving us in the middle of the night after a knock-out-drag-em-down-fight haunted me. I woke up over and over, sweat dripping from my body, and feeling as though I was about to have a heart attack.

Finally around four-thirty or so, I jolted from my bed and started pacing my house until it was time for me to get ready to get to practice. At least it would be an early day. We had a tomorrow. Today's practice was important if we wanted a chance at the Super Bowl. And who wouldn't want that?

I finally just got into my shower to get ready to face the day. On the way out of the house, I gave Dom a call. He didn't pick up the first time. I figured he overslept or something, so I tried calling again.

"Hello?" a gruff, raspy Dom answered the phone.

"Dom?"

"What's wrong?" a female voice just as raspy as Dom's said in the background.

"That didn't take long. Did you find some piece of ass to go home with you?"

He cleared his throat. "No, what's going on, man?"

"Practice?"

"Fuck." He hissed. "I'm up. I'll call you back once I'm on the way," he said then hung up.

I chuckled as I pulled my phone from my ear. "Always playing," I said to myself, shaking my head.

One day he would be brought to his knees by a woman who will be his everything. That poor girl–Soumaya. She never stood a chance. All Dom wanted was instant gratification. There was no way he would have been faithful to one girl. Monogamy wasn't something he was into.

On the way to practice, my phone rang through on the Bluetooth in my SUV.

Pressing the button on my steering wheel to answer it, I said, "Where did you find her?"

"Find who?" he asked, confused.

"Whoever you fucked last night. I didn't think you were one for bringing a girl back to your place, but if it was your only way..." I said, letting the sentence hang.

"I was with Soumaya. She came over and we had dinner... a little more than dinner, and when you called, you woke us up," he explained.

"Soumaya?"

"Yep. And boy do I have something to tell you."

I scoffed. "What?"

"Your girl. The one that you kissed. Soumaya's sister."

"Yeah?" I asked, getting tired of his stalling.

"Her name is Zee. She's the new PR Manager for the team."

I slammed on the breaks. The tires squealing and smoke coming from the brakes.

"Zeus?" he snapped, sounding worried about me.

"She's our new PR Manager? She was the woman on the phone in the conference?"

"Yes. But wait there's more."

"What the fuck more could there actually be?" I asked, looking for a safe place to pull over.

"Did you find somewhere to stop driving?"

"I'm parked. What the fuck else is there?" I snapped at my best friend.

"They're twins."

"Who?"

"Soumaya and Zee. That's why we thought we had kissed the same girl."

"Twins," I said with amazement.

"Yes. I'm on the way to practice now. And I even got something better for you."

"Fuck me. What else?" I sighed.

"I got Zee's number for you."

"Seriously? How'd you pull that off?" I asked, finally able to get back onto the road.

"Technically, I took it from Soumaya's phone when she was asleep."

"How'd that happen?"

"I fucked her until she was so exhausted she went to sleep. Then, I got her phone, got the number, and put her phone back where I found it before she woke back up."

"Sneaky," I said, "you know she'll find out."

"The only way she'd find out is if you told her, and you'd never do that to me."

"That's right, brother. And I'd never do that to you."

Once we hung up, I got back on the road, but all I could think about was that it all made sense now. The fact that Ms. Williams was that woman on the phone, and I didn't even know it. I was that close to her, and she rejected me. At least now there's another reason why. Fuck, if Conway found out... I wouldn't even know where to start with it. Could I even date her? When the hell was she going to tell me? It's not like she could hide it forever.

I pulled into a space and got my bag out. Some of the guys were already changing for practice.

"Did you see the new chick go into Coach's office?" Andy Barbarra asked.

"Yeah, she's a hot one. That skirt was tight," Ralph Nickerson said.

"Who?" I asked.

"This sweet little mocha latte came walking through in heels and one of those skirts that has a slit up the back," Andy said, bringing his fingers to his lips and motioning a chef's kiss. "Whoever she is, she's going to be the next Mrs. Andy Barbarra."

We all laughed.

Andy was a true player. He has had five wives. Zero kids. But he has said he's been in love with every single one of them. Thank God for prenups. None of the women even lasted a year. I think his longest marriage was about three months. Every time he finds a woman, he falls magically in love, and she has to be his soul mate. *The real deal.*

"I could see her signing a prenup for me," he joked.

He knew it was a bad idea. Coach has basically forbidden him from marrying another random girl. They all turn out in heartbreak for Andy.

"Ain't no one ever gonna sign anything for your stankass," Matt Whitley teased.

They snapped their shirts at each other and chased one another around the locker room.

Just because I knew what I knew, I started wondering if the woman they had seen was *my* Zee.

"What did she look like?" I asked.

"Didn't you hear me, tight skirt?" Ralph said.

"Dumbass," I said under my breath in jest. The rest of the guys chuckled with me. "Her face. What did *she* look like? Not her skirt."

"Oh, yeah, that was *fine* too," he said, stroking the sides of his face.

"You're ridiculous, man."

The door opened just then, and Dom came storming

through.

"You're late!" Coach called out.

I didn't even know where he came from. Coach has always been like a ninja. It's as if he's always around, and nobody ever knows when he'll pop up.

"Sorry, I overslept. But I'm here now," he said.

"We know why you 'overslept'," Ralph said, putting his finger up in quotations for overslept.

"Fuck off." Dom hissed, going over to his locker and starting to get ready for practice.

Luckily, his locker was next to mine.

"How was last night?" I asked with a smirk on my face.

"Fucking phenomenal," he replied. "Soumaya is everything I've ever wanted in a girl."

"Sounds like you're hooked," I said.

He put his hand up to his heart and swayed animatedly, "I am."

I chuckled. "I'm happy for you."

"Thanks. Me too," he said with the biggest smile I've seen on his face.

"Can you explain what the fuck is going on?" I asked.

He chuckled. "Yeah, I wouldn't have believed it if I hadn't seen it first-hand."

"I think she's here today," I said quietly, leaning toward him.

"Text her," he said, nodding toward my phone.

"No." I scoffed.

"Yes. Text her something she has no choice but to text you back."

I picked up my phone and tapped on the contact he sent me for Zee.

I tapped out a message, and before I could think twice, I sent it.

Me: I got your number. I kissed you on New Year's Eve at Double Down. Let's get together.

My message went to read and then those dots started

moving. She was going to text me back. I waited and waited, but after a few minutes, I didn't have much hope.

"Anything?" he asked.

I shook my head.

"Well, she said she would talk to you."

I felt the skip of my heart when he said it. Feeling that nearly kicked my ass to the field.

"Ladies, stop your jabbering and get out to the field," he said then clapped to get us going.

———

Once I'd gotten showered and changed, I was able to check my phone. There was a notification.

Zee: I need to speak with you.

My fingers never moved so fast.

Me: When and where?

"Did she respond?" Dom asked, coming up behind me.

"You were right. She wants to talk."

"That's good. Now you just have to be your loveable self," he said, reaching to pinch my cheek, but I dodged him.

He laughed. "Man, just think of it. We could be brothers... in law."

I shook my head. "Just because you've got some deal with your girl doesn't mean that the one I want is going to be just as easy."

"You think that was easy?"

"Nothing in your life is that easy," I replied.

A ping stole my attention from Dom.

Zee: There's a coffee house called Grounds about 5 minutes away. Meet me there in 30 minutes.

I stood there staring at my phone for a long time while I thought about how close I was to getting to see her again. We'd have to meet either way, but at least this way, I could hold some power in the situation.

"Is that her?" Dom asked.

I sighed. "Yeah."

I looked up at him from my phone. The silent question was there.

"She's going to meet me at Grounds."

"That's great," he said, patting me once on the back. "Right?"

"Yeah, no, it is," I replied, looking from my phone back to him. "I don't even know what to say to her."

"Don't say anything. Just let her talk. If there ends up being something between the two of you, then there does."

I took a deep breath. "You're right."

"I know I am. You got this, Buddy."

I sat in my SUV outside of Grounds and watched as customer after customer walked in and out the front door. I hadn't seen her walk in while I sat there. I thought I was being stood up. That was until I saw her. She pulled into the parking lot like a bat out of hell. When she got out of her little car, she hurried toward the door. Her professional gray pencil skirt peeking out from her coat was exactly how the guys had described it.

She looked over her shoulder and then smoothed her hands over the front of her coat. I opened my door to hop out and catch up with her. Just as she reached for the front door, I grabbed it and opened the door for her. When she looked up, her eyes met mine.

"Hi," I said, giving her a wide smile.

"H-hi," she stuttered.

"How about we go inside?" I offered when she didn't move.

She nodded and then walked inside. We went up to the counter. She purposely tried to keep from looking at me, which only made me smirk.

"What can I get you?" the young girl behind the register asked.

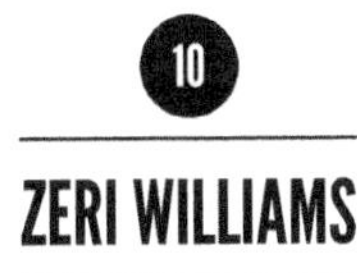

ZERI WILLIAMS

hat a loaded question. I wanted him. I could feel the moment he had come up behind me. I really hadn't wanted it to be true, but then there he was. My entire body had heated and lit up as if a shot of adrenaline had been coursing through my veins. Everything in my brain went blank. It made my entire body halt in its tracks. It was Zeus who had made me need to physically move. He had herded me into the coffee shop. I stood at the counter looking up at the vast menu when the girl asked me what I wanted. I wanted Zeus.

"Caramel latte," I said.

"What size?"

"Medium, please."

"And for you?" she asked Zeus, looking at him with stars in her eyes.

"Large black dark roast."

"Alright," she said then gave us the total.

I pulled my card from my slim crossbody purse at the same time Zeus handed her cash. She looked back and forth between the two of us.

"Cash is always easier," he said, moving the cash to emphasize it.

I rolled my eyes.

She took the cash.

"Feel good about yourself?" I mumbled under my breath.

"Yes. I'm going to consider this our first date."

The girl smirked while she made change at her drawer. She handed the change back to him and then said, "We'll get those drinks right out."

We walked toward the end of the counter where they'd hand us our drinks and waited. I tried not to look at him, but I could feel his eyes on me.

"Here you go," the girl said, setting the drink near us.

"Thank you," we both said, reaching for our respective cups.

"How about over here?" Zeus said, pointing toward a table away from the window where people could walk by and see us. I appreciated that more than he could ever know. I didn't like my business to be out there, and even meeting him in public was pushing all PR rules.

I nodded.

He pulled out the chair for me and then went around to the other side of the table. I felt a little awkward as I tried to figure out where I wanted to start. I knew I needed to talk to him either way.

I took a deep breath and wrapped my hands around my latte. "I think I need to explain things," I started.

He nodded.

I couldn't quite meet his eyes, but I felt those beautiful chocolate brown eyes on me.

"Bill Conway hired me about a month ago. I wasn't even supposed to meet you guys until later in the season. But he had asked me to go to Double Down and make sure it'd be a clean night. We didn't have access to the VIP, but I saw several of your teammates over the balcony," I explained, licking my lips and then looking up into his eyes. "I didn't even know you were you."

"Does that have to change how we first met?" Zeus asked.

I sighed. "It has to. I work for Bill Conway. I'm supposed to protect you from just this kind of scandal."

"I didn't realize that I was a scandal."

"Not you, the fact that I personally work for the owner and you are on the team. Don't you see how that could affect my job?" I nearly pleaded with him.

"No," he said.

I just stared at him. How the hell was I supposed to respond to that? If he didn't see how this could affect my job, he could never understand.

"Look, you're talking about something that hasn't even happened. I know for a fact that only someone so concerned with what might happen to their job would take extra care of handling their relationship."

Relationship? I swallowed hard. What exactly was he asking for? It's one thing to acknowledge what happened; it's another to continue it.

"I'm not here to try to force you into anything you don't want to do, but there *was* something between us. It was like the moment we saw each other, there was no stopping it from happening."

My heart pounded. What the hell? Was this man making me want him with all of his flowery language and singular dimple on his left cheek? That's right, one singular dimple. It must have revolted and said, "I will be noticed!"

"Zee?"

I cleared my throat. "I need to explain." Yes, that's why I asked him to meet me. I looked up into those chocolate eyes and nearly melted from my core. "This is my first *real* job. I need this job. I can't be intertwined with any of the players in any personal way. Having Soumaya and D'Angelo together can get bad. We look so similar that they're already going to be a problem," I said, looking at him and then down, chewing on my lip and then avoiding eye contact.

"I'll admit that you look very similar to your sister. I first thought it was you," he said, clearing his throat with an awkward cough.

"You saw the photograph?"

"Yeah, Dom spoke to me about it. He really likes your sister."

I nearly snorted. "I don't believe that."

"Why?"

"Since this all started, I've reviewed his file. He's had scandal after scandal involving woman after woman. The man's a manwhore."

Zeus barked out a laugh. "He is a little bit. We all have been at one time or another in our careers."

"That doesn't change what's happening right now. He's going to break her heart. I'm going to have to explain this entire situation to Bill, and I'm probably going to lose my job."

"You said this was your first *real* job? How old are you?" he asked, tapping on the side of his coffee cup.

"We just turned twenty-three."

"Twenty-three?"

"Yes," I replied, looking at him for any tells.

"I'll be thirty in a few months," he said as if my age was a deterrent for him.

"Okay."

He took a sip from his cup and watched me. After it had been quiet for far too long, he tapped his cup on the table and then finally spoke. "You know it would make sense for you to at least get to know me. Besides the fact that you work for the team and we'll be spending time together, your sister is kinda dating my best friend. If you want the scandal to never show up, then get out in front of it." He eyed me for a long minute before he said, "You know that the story that Dom and your sister was introduced through you. It could line up really great if you get out in front of it."

I rolled my eyes. He wasn't wrong. It could work. Build the history for the relationship. I pursed my lips. "Do you know if there is anyone that could come out saying he's slept with them in the last few months?"

His mouth wobbled like a blowfish. That would be a clear, concise yes.

It wouldn't be good if some woman came forward spouting out truths and making the tabloids go crazy. That would be the end of the charade.

"There was only one," he tried to explain.

"That you know of," I responded.

Zeus looked sheepishly for a moment. He was more than likely hiding something. I was a pretty good judge of character.

"What?" I asked point blank.

"I may have known he was crushing on a girl but made him go out with me a few times."

"Crushing? Soumaya said she had met him just before Christmas. He's gone out a *few* times since then?"

I caught them. Nothing like that would help the already rampant rumors and bad press for D'Angelo and the team. I watched him carefully. There wasn't necessarily any tells he was stressed or lying, but he definitely was hesitant about telling me whatever it was.

"I-I'm not really sure," he said, stuttering through.

"You're not sure or you don't want to tell me the truth?" I snapped.

While he was trying to figure out what to say, I decided I was done.

I shook my head and then said, "I'm done. I told you what happened and was truthful with you. When you decide you can do the same, you can come find me," I said, getting up with my coffee and walking out.

Back in my car, I drove straight home. Soumaya wasn't home yet. She must have had a lot of Retriever items requested. That's actually really good. With each order, she receives a little extra plus there are regularly tips. Her clients loved her.

I sent her a quick message just to check in.

Me: I'm back home. How's today going?

It took her a lot longer to respond than normal, but I eventually heard the notification.

Soumaya: Going good. I sent a message out to all my clients letting them know they'd be seeing a new team manager in their profile and that they'd be taken care of by other Retrievers for the next couple of days, assuring them that their privacy is in the best hands and I would see them all soon.

Me: Good. Let me know when I need to pick you up.

Soumaya: I think I should be done around 5:30.

Me: I'll be there.

We were going to have to buy another car soon with us going in opposite directions most of the day. I doubt she will be able to drop me off and then go to work. Besides the fact that I'll probably need to leave the office at some point. I'm going to need to build my relationships with news media.

I opened my laptop and started searching for another car. With luck, we'd find something affordable that wasn't a complete lemon.

The cheapest car, worth anything, was still ten grand. It'd take a chunk of our already depleted savings. I'd talk to Soumaya about it and see if she can swing paying me back for half. That's how we bought our first car and the one we have now. I'm just a better driver. Soumaya has backed into a bench before.

I went over to the couch, pulled my leg up under me, and then set my laptop and put on a romcom on Netflix. Has anyone else noticed that the big studios have basically stopped making romantic comedy movies? Netflix has been turning them out one after another, and they're not all that great. But the ones that follow the romance tropes like workplace romance, enemies to lovers, and who can forget the foreign country meeting a hot man with a sexy accent while trying to prove herself. That's one of my favorites—even if they're predictable.

About halfway through, I heard my phone ping with a new notification. I paused the movie and reached over to look at my phone.

Unknown Number: I'm sorry I felt like I couldn't be honest with you. But I want to. Can we try again in a less public place?

I scoffed. "Yeah, good try."

My fingers started typing before I thought it through.

Me: You can say you're sorry, but it's still not going to change the situation we are currently dealing with.

After I pressed send, I almost regretted it, but I couldn't go into my new position with the Scavengers not expecting the truth and respect. All he did was waste my time.

11

LUTHER 'ZEUS' ZEUSES

"Should have fucking seen that coming," I said to myself. She was a fucking lion, expecting the most from people and never getting it. I wish I could have been honest with her. It could have changed the entire dialogue between us.

I had been sitting at my desk in my office at Olympus Gym for over an hour when I finally decided to stop being a pansy and text her. I almost wish I hadn't. I needed to tell her I was sorry either way, and maybe the next time we see each other, it will be under different circumstances.

I started tapping my fingers on my desk while I tried to figure out what I could do to get back into the good graces of Zeri Williams.

Three hours later, I still didn't have anything good.

"Hey boss," Denis started as he leaned into my office.

I looked up in a confused daze.

"Whoa, you okay?" he asked.

I sighed. "Yeah, I'm fine."

I could tell he didn't believe me. I wouldn't have either. I wasn't doing a good job trying to look normal. That woman had me completely turned upside down and then sideways.

I cleared my throat. "There's a girl."

Denis chuckled. "Isn't there always?"

"Yeah, but this one is different. She's independent, and she doesn't just put up with my shit. She argues back. Almost like she debates me, and I can't come up with answers because I've never had to."

"She sounds different. They're normally falling over themselves to get to spend one night with you." Before I could speak again, he followed it up with, "I don't get it... I'm so much hotter than you."

I barked out a laugh. "It's probably the millions attached to my name."

"It does add to your resume."

"It does. It just so happens this one doesn't care about the money. She's got her own thing, and she's got morals," I said with astonishment.

"Morals?"

I chuckled. "Yeah," bringing my hand up to scratch at my jaw, "she has this way of making me want to be better." I sat there thinking about that for a moment.

"Isn't that a good thing?" Denis asked.

"Yes." I chuckled. "It is."

"So, what are you going to do about it?"

"I'm going to make this girl mine," I said, getting up from my chair and grabbing all of my things. I started closing up for the day.

"You good, Zeus?"

"I'm going to figure out how to get my girl, and I've got some online stalking to do."

He laughed.

I turned off the lights to my office with him still inside, laughing in the chair.

Once I got out into my SUV, I immediately called Dom.

"What's up?" he answered.

"I need you to get me all the information you can on your girl's sister."

He sighed. "What happened?"

"I may not have handled the situation properly."

"And?" he asked, trying to get me to tell him.

"I told her that you and I basically have fucked other girls not so long ago."

"You're a fucking idiot. How am I supposed to get out of that? You know she's going to tell Soumaya everything."

"I understand that, but she walked out on me."

"What the hell do you think Soumaya's going to do to me? I need to get out in front of this."

"No, man, come on, you've got to help me."

"I've already helped. So much so that if my girl were to find out I got her sister's number for you from her phone, she'd probably castrate me. Do you understand how close they are? They're fucking twins. They basically use telepathy to communicate."

I laughed. "You know that's not real, right?"

I wouldn't doubt they could communicate on some level without physically talking to each other. But Dom and I have been doing something like this for years. A grunt, eyebrow raise, or head nod was all it would take and I'd know exactly what to do without alerting anyone else. We were good like that. I'm sure Zee and her sister were even closer.

"Never mind. I don't want you to get into trouble with her. But at least do me a favor..."

"What's that?"

"Keep your ear out if she starts talking to you about it. Just let me know what I can do to fix it."

"Sure. Um, yeah, let me let you go."

"She's there, isn't she?" I asked.

"Yep, I'll talk to you later."

"Yeah, okay, see ya, man," I said.

He just hung up.

He was a total goner over this one. I might end up losing my best friend to a woman he could fall in love with. That hadn't sat with me very well. I didn't like the idea of not having an all access pass to him. We'd done everything together for years, and it was different now.

When I got home, I sat down on the couch and turned on *Goodfellas*, one of the best movies out there in my opinion. However, it wasn't holding my attention. I kept picking up my phone and checking my messages as if Zeri would just out of the blue text me after the fantastic impression I left on her.

Huffing, I opened social media and started looking for her.

Nothing. "What the fuck else would she go by?"

I searched for Z Williams. And when nothing came up, I tried to search for her sister's name. However, not knowing how to spell it came into the equation. Maybe she would be Googleable. Going to Google, I did a search for Zeri and added Pittsburgh Scavengers to the search.

"FUCKING HELL! Goddamn nothing." I tossed my phone to the other end of my couch. Blowing a deep breath through my nose in frustration, I reached for my phone again.

Zeus: Why don't you have social media?

I pressed send and then just watched my phone until I saw that she read it. I waited while watching Robert De Niro in one of his best roles of his career. Just as I was getting back into the movie, I heard a notification ping.

A little nervous, but excited that she texted me back, I lifted my phone to see that it was not Zeri.

Mom: What time are you coming over for dinner?

Zeus: I don't know. I might skip tonight.

My mom dialed my number approximately point zero four seconds after she read my message.

"Hi, Mom," I said with a happy sigh.

"What do you mean you're not coming? I'm making chicken fried steak, baked potatoes, and all your favorite greens."

My tongue literally sat up panting.

"I figured you had something good happening in your kitchen."

"I sure do. Now why are you trying to get out of coming over?"

"I'm just not feeling it."

"Well, why the hell not? Are you sick?"

"No, I'm not sick. I just..."

"What did you do?" she snapped at me.

"I may have not been truthful with this girl I like and she called me out on my shit."

"Don't curse."

"Sorry," I said, apologetically.

"Do you like this girl?"

I sighed. "I probably wouldn't even be telling you if I didn't."

"That's a good point. I never know what you're off doing... or who."

"Mom," I pleaded.

"Oh, fine. You still have to come help eat what I'm fixin'— girl or not."

Before I could answer, I heard an incoming call. *Who the hell could that be?* I pulled my phone from my ear, still hearing inaudible words coming from my mom to see that it was Zeri.

"Hey Mom, I've got to go. She's calling me."

"Call me back."

"Okay," I said, switching over to Zeri's call. "Hey."

An exasperated sigh came through the line. "Look, if you think by continuing to text me that you're going to get anywhere with me, you should just know I'm not that forgiving."

I wanted to laugh but restrained myself. "But you did call me back."

"I did to tell you to stop. This isn't professional."

"No, it's personal. We had a connection. I'm sorry I couldn't be completely honest, but I'm going to be from here on out, and you know the truth anyways."

"It's still not going to work. We can just be friends." Then she rushed to say, "Professionally."

"I would rather be friends. Especially since your sister and my best friend seem to be getting close."

"Yep. That's what they're supposed to be doing. It looks better for the media."

"Speaking of, why don't you have any social media accounts?"

"I do. They're just private. My services are done through a different account but only if I need social media. I find using the bigger outlets will get your message out, and that's when people will make their opinions and post to their accounts. You can't control those narratives, but you can control how you react to them."

"That's true," I conceded.

The line was too quiet for too long. I didn't really know what to say. She thought quickly on her feet and was eloquent while doing it.

"Luther," she sighed, "why are we doing this?"

I scoffed, "Because we need to give this a shot."

The moan of frustration that came through the phone made me inch to the edge of my couch with anticipation.

"How about we start over?" I offered.

She audibly inhaled so deeply I thought she might actually say something. When she didn't, I tried again.

"I'm not a bad guy. You should at least give me a chance since we're going to be working together."

"Fine," she replied, exasperated, "we'll start over."

"Good. My name is Zeus."

"I like Luther more," she stated bluntly.

I chuckled. "Alright, you can call me Luther. And what do I call you?"

"Hmm, that's actually a difficult decision. At work you

should use Ms. Williams, and you can call me Zee when I see you outside of work."

"I don't know. I would rather be able to call you Zee all of the time."

"No. I want to keep everything professional. It would only make sense the rest of your team sees us as professional friends. That's what I can give you."

"If that's all you can give, I'll take it."

"Good, I can't keep doing this with you."

"I don't know why not. I'm having a lot of fun."

"I'm done for today. If you need to speak with me, you can schedule an appointment."

She hadn't given me the opportunity to say anything else before I heard the call end.

I pulled my phone away from my face to check the screen. "Yep, she definitely hung up on me."

Me being a smartass, I instantly pulled up the message thread with her and sent her another text message.

Zeus: Let's work on you hanging up on me for the future. I don't really feel like that's a good way to be professional.

I watched as those little dots moved over and over without response. She must have been *pisssssed*. Which only made me chuckle harder. I wouldn't be getting to her if she didn't care. I truly believed she was having just as hard of a time not liking me as I was trying to stop pushing for her to give in to me.

12

ZERI WILLIAMS

"AHHH! That man!" I slammed my phone down on the table, only to pick it back up and double check to make sure I hadn't broken the screen. "Why do I let him get to me?"

I was sure if Soumaya was here, she'd tell me it was because I liked him. She wouldn't be wrong. I thought there was something almost magical as he walked across the club floor toward me. Then there was that kiss. I barely touched my lips with the tips of my fingers, remembering how he kissed me. I felt it in my toes; it was so good.

Figuring my sister wouldn't be home for another couple of hours, I went into my bedroom and opened up my nightstand drawer. I pulled out my favorite boyfriend substitution. Slipping out of my clothes, I got into bed and then pulled my covers up. I pressed the on, letting the *bzz* go to a solid *bzzzzzzz*—because who actually likes the *bzz bzz* or *bzz...bzbz...bzzz*? I lowered it in my hand under the cover, finding the exact spot I needed to get a little excitement happening. Then I closed my eyes and imagined every inch of Zeus. I made sure I'd memorized enough to keep me going.

Just as my jellybean was getting ready to party, I got a notification on my phone. Sighing, I picked up my phone and looked at it.

Dad: Don't forget we're having lunch tomorrow. Please remind your sister.

That's one way to kill the mood. "Fuck my life." My happy ending was just out of reach thanks to me checking my phone. I shouldn't have done it, but I did.

Zee: Of course. We will be there.

Dad: Good. Because last time it was awkward sitting there waiting for you both to show up.

I wrapped my covers over me and dropped my feet off of my bed. There was no way I was finishing now.

Zee: Dad, I promise we will be there.

Dad: Good. See you tomorrow.

Zee: See you tomorrow.

I opened up my messages with Soumaya and started typing.

Zee: Are you coming back tonight?

I waited for her to respond, but when I didn't get a response in ten minutes, I went to get into the shower. Whenever Soumaya wasn't here, I always spent an extra-long time under the stream of hot, steamy water. It felt so good to stand under the water. Especially since I was still a little worked up and nowhere to go.

When I got out, I wrapped my towel around me and walked to my room. I checked my phone to see a new message from Soumaya.

Soumaya: Dom wants me to stay the night.

I quickly started texting her back.

Zee: We have lunch with Dad tomorrow. You better be there.

The dots started moving quickly as I waited for her to ask me to come pick her up. I knew she wouldn't want Dom to meet Dad yet or even at all. Dad would hate the idea of her dating a player like Dom. God, he would hate the idea of me dating someone like Luther. He wouldn't think he was good enough for either of us. He would say, *"Players will be players."* He wouldn't be wrong. Not with what I've seen and know now.

Soumaya: Can you actually come get me?

Zee: Fine. It will be like 45 minutes.

Soumaya: Thanks!

I rolled my eyes and went over to my dresser to get a pair of plaid flannel pajamas and soft sweatshirt. I grabbed my wallet and keys from my purse and made sure to lock up our apartment. I hated driving at night into the ritzy area of Pittsburgh. I felt like we stuck out. Which we did. It's odd enough seeing twins, but adult twins people always stare, and then to make it all even worse, the glares we get for being interracial–it makes your skin crawl to see people hate you for no reason other than what you look like.

I pulled into the gated neighborhood and rolled down my window. I showed the guy my ID, and he checked me off the list quickly. Dom must have added me onto the list.

I pulled onto Dom's driveway and sent a text message to Soumaya.

Zee: I'm outside. Hurry up.

Soumaya: Just saying goodbye. I'll be right out.

"Sure you will," I said to myself.

It was nearly five minutes later when Soumaya came walking out with Dom right on her heels. He opened the door for her, waved hello to me, and then leaned in and kissed her before saying goodbye to her for what had to be the sixtieth time.

He even stood on his driveway until after I backed off.

"Wow, what the hell is actually happening here?" I asked.

"I don't know, but it's fun," she said, pulling down the sun visor and looking at her face.

I looked over from the corner of my eyes. "Is that a freaking hickey?" I asked, moving her hair back from her neck.

"I guess so," she said, proudly.

"You let him mark you?"

"Jeez, relax."

"Soumaya, we're seeing Dad in less than fifteen hours. I can't believe you. It's just like when we were teenagers. You'd be sneaking in through the window while I had to cover for you."

"Well, you're a real downer tonight."

"No, I'm up, bringing you home so that you don't miss lunch with Dad and I have to see him hurt by you again."

We stayed silent the rest of the way home until I unlocked our apartment and we went our separate ways. She called over the balcony toward me to get my attention.

"Hey, Zee?"

"Yeah?"

"I'm sorry."

I sighed. "I know. Me too."

"Goodnight."

"Night," I said before walking into my room.

I closed the door to my room and got under the covers. I was done with the day and just wanted to wake up tomorrow to start it all over.

I woke to my alarm and immediately turned it off. I laid back down on my pillow and stared up at my ceiling. I really didn't want to deal with the day. It felt like everything I worked for was slipping through my fingers. I hated not being able to be in control of things, and Soumaya never wants to be in control of anything, so she doesn't have to take responsibility for anything.

I heaved myself up out of bed and basically stumbled to the bathroom. I splashed some water on my face. By the time I was done, Soumaya was already at the door knocking.

"Almost done," I called out.

"Okay. Can I come in?"

"Yep."

She opened the door and came into the bathroom with me. She went straight to the toilet and sat down.

"I really like him," she said.

"I think you like the sex," I replied with a bit of sass.

"That happens to be a *big* positive."

We both giggled.

"As long as he's good to you."

"He is. I think you'd be surprised how good of a guy he actually is."

"Maybe."

"I think Zeus might be a good guy too. Maybe you should give him a shot."

She flushed the toilet and then turned on the water for the shower.

"Sou, I don't want to give some guy who can't be honest about the simplest of things a chance." I looked at her through the bathroom mirror. "You remember when Uncle Craig got found out?"

"Oh God, yeah, he lied every chance he could get. That one woman who came up pregnant..."

"Exactly. It's a good thing that Aunt Lily handled that like a boss."

"Right. I think kicking his lying ass to the curb was the best thing she ever did. Besides, I like Derrick," Soumaya said.

"I do too. He's good for her. As long as she lets him."

"I think Zeus is different. Dom was telling me what an amazing guy Zeus is."

"If he's so amazing, then why does he have to go around with a nickname for a Greek god? Conceited much?"

"Oh my God, Zee, are you mad he has a nickname that literally correlates to his last name?" she asked as she put moisturizer on her face.

"No."

"You are. Wow, talk about conceited."

"I'm not being conceited. I'm anything but conceited," I said, feeling cornered about my opinions.

"Look, Zee, Zeus is a nice guy. He's known Dom since they were little. Apparently, Zeus' mom worked for Dom's family, and they were all really good friends," She said then brought her finger up to her lip and tapped a few times thinking.

"What?"

"It's kinda funny."

"What's funny?"

"Zee and Zeus. Z isn't a common letter for names, and you both have Zs—it's fate."

I barked out a laugh. "Fate?" I scoffed.

"Yes, fate. Wouldn't it be interesting if I dated Dom and you dated his best friend?" Soumaya said, daydreaming of some sort of fairytale that will never happen with those playboys.

"No, it wouldn't be interesting. It'd be impossible. They're players."

"Riiiight?" she said, looking at me confused. "You know they play for the team you work for, right?"

"I meant players like they go out all the time sleeping with a different woman every night."

"Dom told me everything. He didn't expect to even see me again. He saw me when I delivered groceries to Makenna Cooper. He's her brother. I'm not mad that he was with someone else. We found each other, and he *showed* me exactly how much he wanted me."

I didn't reply to her but thought about what she had said. Dom was honest with her. I hadn't thought he would have been honest.

"What about you? Don't you like Zeus? I bet he'd be fun to tango with," Soumaya said, waggling her eyebrows at me.

I knew he'd be fantastic in bed. I'd been thinking about it since our kiss. But when I figured out who he was, I had to focus on everything I needed to do for Soumaya. I couldn't help but think about how Luther lit up my very being. I just couldn't let him get close—not when I've done everything I've done to get to where I am at my age. It's an achievement. I know that, and I don't want to let it go. I want to prove to everyone, the doubter, naysayers, and even myself that I can do this. Even if I didn't feel like I was ready, my father would always tell me, if I didn't have the opportunity in front of me, then I wouldn't be ready, but with the opportunity of a lifetime right in front of me, I knew I was ready.

"I thought I liked him, but I can't..."

"Why not? Come on, Zee. I think you'd really like him. That is if you gave him a chance."

"I can't give him a chance. I work for the team. Nope. *And* I'm done talking about this. So just leave it alone, okay?"

"Fine, fine," she said, putting her hands up in the air. "I won't bring him up again."

"Thank you," I said with a sigh. "What are you wearing today?"

"What? You don't want to dress alike?" she said, dripping in sarcasm.

"Let's not."

"You're still coming to my art show tonight, right?" she asked with a mouth full of toothpaste.

"Of course. I can't wait to be there to support you. Who do you think will be there?"

"Critics. Other artists. Potentially some collectors."

"It would be really cool to sell one of your paintings."

"I'm not banking on it. But it is really good exposure for me. And I was able to sneak in a photo I retouched with oils."

"The one of downtown?"

"Yep," she said, taking a heavy breath.

"I love that one. Did you make prints?"

"Yeah, I've got it saved. You know I get them scanned every time I show something. I barely had enough to cover it this time with what I'm making at Retriever."

"You know I'll cover that kind of thing."

"I know... but I need to take care of myself."

"We take care of each other," I said, pulling her into my side and hugging her tightly.

"Always and forever," she whispered.

"Always and forever," I whispered back.

![13]

LUTHER 'ZEUS' ZEUSES

I knew I'd wear her down.

I watched as Zee came walking down to the field, Coach and another guy at her side, and her professional mannerisms making my cock hard.

"What's wrong with you?" Jeremiah Sutton asked when he passed me my water bottle and I didn't catch it. He looked where my attention had been drawn, and there was zero chance of me taking my eyes off her while she was on the field. "Whoa, who's that?"

Mine.

The word pulsed through my body with every heartbeat. I had already decided I was going to do whatever I needed to do to get her in my bed and beside me. There was this crazy pull to her. Was this what it felt like to find your soulmate?

"Zeri Williams. The new PR Manager," I said casually.

"Oh, is she doing damage control for Dom?"

"Yeah. She's good. I haven't seen anything else about it, and all the tabloid outlets dropped the story. I even think I heard they were going after the guy who originally sold the photo."

"Damn, she's good. I'm glad she's on our side."

"Yeah, " I chuckled, "she's kinda a spitfire."

"Nice. Spicy and sexy. I like it."

"Hey," I growled, "off limits."

Jer chuckled. "I don't see a ring."

"No, but you do see who she's walking with. You know the rules—no head office staff."

"Is she head office?" he asked, a slight squeak in his tone as if to say, *"But is she really off limits?"*

"Yes," I said with a flatness to my tone.

"Somebody sounds overprotective," he muttered under his breath as he walked off.

I wasn't being overprotective. I was a normal amount of overprotective. I was just making sure that my best friend's girl's sister was in good hands. There wasn't any reason other than that for why I was acting protective and maybe even a little possessive.

Everyone started to gather around when Coach walked onto the field.

"Gather close," Coach said, motioning us closer. "This is Zeri Williams. You may have seen her walking around the last few days. She is our new PR Manager. This does not mean you can go out and test her skills," Coach joked.

We all chuckled.

"I'm serious. I need you to be on your best behavior. Ms. Williams will be on field and available during your action photos next week with Viktor Cozcroft."

"What kind of action shots are we doing this year?" Camden Durkes asked.

"We're doing a mixture. We've got to update the website and social medias. Expect at least thirty minutes apiece."

Groans circled around the group. Thirty minutes with someone telling you how to pose and what to do was exhausting. We did action and profile photos early last year when we got a few new players. Some of them aren't even with our team anymore.

"Get over it," Coach called out.

We chuckled.

"This is your opportunity to do a PR checkup and get your photos done. I'll call you over, one at a time, to schedule a block of time this next week. Viktor, how about you come over first?"

We all oohed at him like he got called to the principal's office.

Dom came walking over while Coach started with Viktor. "What's up, man?"

"Nothing. Just tryin' to get through the day at this point," I replied. "How's it going with your girl?"

"Soumaya? It's Su-my-ah." He enunciated her name so I would use it instead of calling her his girl.

"Alright, I got it. Su-my-ah. How's it going with Soumaya?"

"She's good. Actually, I think I've got a plan for us."

"Us?" I questioned.

"Yes, us. My guy got tickets to Soumaya's art show."

I furrowed my brow. An art show. Who in the hell would want to go to an art show? Not me, that's for sure.

"Soumaya is in an exclusive art show, and she's taking her sister as her plus one."

That piqued my interest. Anytime I could see Zee outside of the field was exactly where I wanted to be. But an art show.

"I don't know a ton about the show, but Soumaya is nervous, and I want to make sure she has some support."

"Aww, you're going to be a great ballet dad."

"As Leonard would say, 'Our babies will be smart and beautiful'."

We love *The Big Bang Theory*. We've binged it at least a dozen times. Definitely every off-season. The creators need to do a movie tie-in to close it all out. I want to see them with their kids. I mean seeing them as kids on *Young Sheldon* was fucking amazing, but I still want more. Oh, and can we talk about the fact that Sheldon was allergic to cats, but then when Amy and he break up, he gets a ton of them? Or was I the only one who caught that?

I snort-laughed. "When is this *art* show?"

"Tomorrow," he answered. "Wear a suit, and I'll pick you up at six."

"Damn, do I even get dinner and drinks before I get fucked?" I joked.

"I'm sure they'll have cucumber sandwiches and shit like that," he teased.

"You know you're kinda an asshole."

"But you love me, and you're going to get time with her," he said, looking over his shoulder. "Look, I hate that you felt you couldn't talk about me to Soumaya's sister. I don't want that. I think I'm going to do whatever I can to get her to come to the dark side."

"Really?" I deadpanned.

"You got it," he said, acting cocky.

"DOM!" Coach called out.

Dom smirked at me and jogged off. He was over there longer than anyone else. I watched as he eyed me on and off as he did his thing and charmed *my* girl.

Jeremiah came up to me and said, "Look at him playing. Doesn't he have a girl he's literally tied to until his dick is out of hot water?"

"Yeah," I said, my voice deeper than it should have been.

"ZEUS!" Coach called out.

Dom smirked at me as he took time coming back over to me. "She's feeling feisty today, so be careful. Oh, and us going to the art show is a surprise, so don't fucking tell her."

"Yeah, yeah, okay."

"ZEUS!" Coach repeated.

I jogged over to them. Zee avoided looking at me, while Coach gave me the stink-eye, and that Viktor guy was trying to eye me up as if I were some sort of competition. We might be—I didn't like the way he was looking at her.

"We're hoping to get you on Tuesday. I'm going to put you

down for eleven. But be ready to wait," Zee said, penciling me onto a paper then she turned to Coach and said, "Who's next?"

"Is that all I get?" I asked.

"Do you have a question?" she finally asked, looking up into my eyes.

I felt that connection drawing me to her. There was something there. She knew it too. She was avoiding me because she didn't want to feel it. But it was there. Our lives are going to be intertwined, and all I needed to do was make sure she knew I would be there for her.

"No, no questions. Thank you, Miss Williams."

I saw the slightest jolt of stiffness when I used her last name. That's what she wanted. I was going to make sure she knew I'd keep to her wishes, but I'd also annoy her while doing it—and wear her down.

I smirked as I turned and walked away. I knew I had gotten to her, and it felt good. At this point, all I knew was that I was going to go to her sister's art show, and I was going to look so good that she wouldn't be able to keep her eyes off me.

14

ZERI WILLIAMS

That motherfucker. I don't even know why it bothered me. I told him to be professional.

"Are you okay?" Viktor asked.

"I'm fine. Why?" I asked, trying to play off the awkward tension.

"That seemed like something."

"Nope. I'm really just meeting the players for the first time like you."

"Oh?" he said.

"Yeah, This week was my first week."

"Well, I'm glad I could be here for your first week," he said, flirtatiously.

Viktor was an odd man. At least odd for me. His brown and maroon plaid corduroy pants with brown loafers and a frilly maroon button up under a mink fur coat with three thin gold necklaces. I could have sworn my gay-dar was going off, but if he was flirting, he could be just skirting the line of equal opportunity. I'm all for love of any kind. I just don't like vaginas. I don't even like mine. She has a fucking temper tantrum every month and makes me feel like hell with all the symptoms of PMDD.

As we worked to get the rest of the players scheduled, Viktor continued to make little comments on and off about me. All flirty. But it was when he asked me about my skin color that I had a problem.

"What are you?" he asked.

EXCUSE THE FUCK OUT OF YOU! Nope. That is not okay. You never ask anyone *what they are*. This fucker thought it was okay to do it too.

"You've got a great complexion. I would love to photograph you nude," he said before I could say anything back to him.

"Excuse me?" I said, trying to give him the opportunity to retract his racist comment.

"Your complexion. It's beautiful. I'm guessing you're interracial."

"And you're fucking rude. You don't ask people what they are," I snapped and then walked over to Jared to let him know what just happened.

"Hey, Jared, there's a problem," I started.

He looked confused for a moment but realized I was not happy walking over to him.

"Are you alright?" he asked, now concerned.

"No. I need to file a complaint against Viktor."

"What happened?" he said, looking over my shoulder and then back into my eyes.

"He just asked me what I was and then told me he wanted to photograph me nude."

He was shocked.

"He said he guessed I was interracial, and I told him he was rude and that you never ask people '*what they are*'," I continued to explain.

"Okay, I'm going to start by saying that was wrong of him to do. Let me get in contact with the head office and let them know what happened. Okay?"

I nodded.

"Okay, stay over here with me."

I felt safe with Jared Hobbs. He had the father figure down. He could tell just how upset I was at how I was addressed and described. I zoned out as Jared got on the phone and Luther came walking over.

"Hey, is everything alright?" he asked.

I crossed my arms over my chest, feeling exposed and not making eye contact.

Luther looked over at Coach Hobbs, who was still on the phone. "Coach? What's going on?"

"Don't worry about it right now. Get back to practice, and if there is anything to talk about, I'll make sure we talk," Jared said while on hold on his phone.

"You okay?" Luther asked, looking directly into my eyes, making me feel as though I was stripped naked and only he was the one who could see me.

I nodded. "I'm fine."

He looked as though he wanted to say something else, but instead he sighed and went back out to the field. When I looked up to see him walk away, he went directly over to Dom and started talking. They'd probably get the whole story pretty quickly.

"They want to see him. We don't work with people who make insensitive comments or treat anyone with disrespect. I am so sorry. Do you want me to escort you out?"

"No, I will be fine. Please, will you let me know what happens here?"

"Of course. I'll give you a call in a bit," he said.

"Thanks, Jared."

Leaving from work, I only wanted to do one thing—talk to my sister. But I had to get home and get ready for lunch with my dad. That should be fun. He's never been a big supporter of racist bigots.

As soon as I got back to the apartment, Soumaya was getting ready, but she stopped what she was doing when she saw me. "What the fuck happened?" she asked, putting down her eyeliner.

I sighed, feeling exhausted, and it wasn't even lunchtime.

She stood and walked toward me. "Seriously, what happened?"

As I relayed the entire story, she's standing there with her jaw dropped.

I know football is a predominantly male-based world. But it's also predominantly multiracial. On an active roster, there are fifty-three players. Out of those fifty-three, forty-two of them aren't Caucasian on the Scavengers. A recent study even said that the percentage is about seventy percent players other than Caucasian. There's nothing wrong with that. What the problem is, is that the NFL would recommend a photographer that has views that don't align with the majority of their players.

Never mind the racist behavior, but it's objectifying and sexualizing the only woman he could find. I don't know how they will handle this, but at least Jared took me seriously. Had he acted like so many of my teachers before, where it was the victim's fault, it would have ended differently.

"Are you kidding me? This is the *legendary* photographer the NHL recommends to their teams?" she said, holding up air-quotes up when she said *legendary*.

"I'm not kidding. I wish they could just hire you. You've done kids sports before, and they look like a fifty-year-old experienced photographer took them."

"Thank you?" She said, questioning the compliment.

"Seriously. I think if anyone sees your work and then finds out how young you are, they'd be intimidated. You're brilliant."

"See, that's a much better compliment," she said with a little teasing. "But what are *they* going to do? That man was racist and sexualized you."

"So you don't think I overreacted?" I asked, feeling worried for the first time since it happened that Bill Conway would think I overreacted to the situation.

"Absolutely not. As an artist, I would never address anyone I'd like to photograph like that. That was rude and crass. I would never have acted like that toward anyone I was contracted to work for. It was fucking unprofessional. Period. I hope they fire him."

She made me feel a little bit better, but I've noticed over the years that it's not about what we think—it's about what the majority of other people think. Growing up in a household where you were already criticized for being interracial in society and had to deal with racist comments through even elementary school. Also seeing your parents deal with angry racists saying things that cut hard to the bone. That saying of *sticks and stones can break your bones but words will never hurt* is bullshit. I've seen my mother crying to my father because she wasn't allowed to be part of a church group because she fell in love with my dad. And I've seen my dad have to stand there while black men and women cussed in his face for diluting his genes. Why can't they all just fuck off? Did we really hurt anyone?

So many emotions were flying through my head and heart over this. I didn't want to be fired because I spoke up, and I didn't want to get retaliation from any of the men in the league. I knew I had chosen a tough profession, but I wanted it, and I told myself to go for it. But even with those feelings, it doesn't mean that shit doesn't hurt. It doesn't mean I just need a thicker skin. And it doesn't mean that my concern for my safety doesn't matter.

Every negative thought I had pushed me further and further away from being in a good place.

"Hey," Soumaya said, getting my attention, "I have faith they will handle this situation professionally and properly. Okay?"

I nodded.

"Good, now, let's go get lunch over with so we can have even more awkwardness," she said, making me laugh.

We made it to the diner with ten minutes to spare. Figuring

our dad would be on the way, we went ahead inside and got a table. Not surprisingly, he was already sitting at a table.

"Oh, that's our third," I said to the hostess.

Dad stood and leaned in to hug each of us. "How are my girls doing?"

"We're good, Dad," Soumaya answered first.

"Good, come sit. Tell me everything. Your art show? That's tomorrow, right?" Dad asked.

"Yep. I'm a little nervous."

"Don't be. You're an amazing artist. If somebody doesn't like your work, they must be blind."

"Thanks, Dad. But that's really not how it works. There are going to be critics there to write about the show."

"Again, they've got to be blind," he said, giving me a proud smile. "What are you girls thinking about for lunch?"

I was just glad most of the conversation was all about Sou. I needed a few extra minutes to pull together a fake smile for our dad.

"Maybe the Ruben," Sou said, looking at the menu.

Don't ask me yet. I thought.

"Zee? What about you? Did you see the salmon?" Dad asked.

He had always been really supportive with my diet choices. When I decided to be vegetarian in junior high, he read up on it and then started adjusting dinners at home to give me more options. Then in high school when I went to the doctor and they said I needed more nutrients, I talked with him about what my diet options could be. I went with pescatarian. However, I only eat fish occasionally. Not too often, perhaps once a week, Sou was always getting on to me about eating more protein. I'm actually really bad at eating regularly.

"Oh yeah?" I said.

"Yeah," he said, leaning over to point it out, "it's blackened. You like that, right?"

"I do. But I'm also considering the avocado toast with fried eggs. You know I love avocado."

"I do. And how's your new job going? All those football players treating you with respect?" Dad asked with judgment.

"The players are fine," Soumaya said for me.

"What does that mean? Isn't the guy you were photographed with on the team? That's why you were photographed? Because he's famous?"

Thank God the spotlight went back onto Soumaya. I couldn't deal with anything extra today.

"His name is Dominic. We've been seeing each other for a little bit..."

"How long is a little bit?" Dad said, eyeing her with disapproval.

Of course he knew that we weren't virgins anymore, but seeing it is a totally different story. I'm sure he's been razed about it at work. It's not like he hasn't put our portraits up in his office for the last decade.

"Long enough. You and Mom would approve."

He folded his arms across his chest and frowned. "I won't ever approve of anything before marriage."

"I doubt you'd like for me to marry him first and possibly find out he's not a good guy," she said.

"Is he a good guy? It sounds like he's not."

"No, no, no," Soumaya said, animatedly waving her hands in front of her. "He's really a great guy. He found out when he was an adult his dad had a whole other family and he accepted his half-sister as if she'd been there his entire life. I haven't met her, but she owns *Sugar Mama's*. And he's a great uncle."

Dad eyed her.

"I swear. And he's really smart too."

"Just how old is this Dominic?" Dad asked.

I was so happy I wasn't in the hot seat today. Our dad has always been inquisitive when it came to our boyfriends. I remember junior prom. He wanted them to come in and 'have a conversation' with him. We found out that Dad had told them whatever they do to us, he'll do to them. That's extremely scary coming from a six-foot-four, three hundred pound man.

I still have zero clue how Dad landed a hottie like Mom. She's the cutest five-foot-four ginger you've ever seen. I accidentally overheard him call her his personal pocket pussy. I'm still talking about it in therapy. And when we were young, Dad and Grandpa got into it, and Dad called him a leprechaun. It took three years before Grandpa talked to Dad again. So basically what I'm saying is that Dad never thinks before he speaks.

"He's older than me," she said, nervously.

I couldn't remember how old he was. I was still making my way through all fifty-three player's profiles.

"How much older?" Dad said, sternly.

"About ten years," She replied, meekly.

Dad inhaled sharply. "Ten?"

Luther was the same age. I remembered that. Just another reason Luther wouldn't be a good choice for me.

"Yes, but aren't you always wanting me to be with someone more responsible? Well, he is."

Dad leaned back in his chair and crossed his arms over his chest. "How responsible can the man be for putting you into that kind of situation in a public place?"

He's not wrong, but I'm team Soumaya all the way. I think she's taken enough heat at this point for me.

"Dad, he really is a good guy. Once he found out that this photo was out there in the world, he contacted us to get the legal started so she wouldn't be exposed further. He's also a big humanitarian. I read in his file he gives his time and money to rescues and animal shelters so that they don't spend their entire lives in a cage, and he keeps the shelters no kill."

Dad was a sucker for an animal lover. That's one reason Mom always came home with a different pet to foster until they could find their forever homes. He loved her for her big heart.

"Fine, okay. I'll leave him alone for now. Just no more scandalous pictures. Your poor mother has been dealing with those church ladies all week. Martha's the worst."

Soumaya and I snickered.

Once we were done eating, we did our standard goodbyes with the big bear hugs, and Dad whispered into my ear, "He's probably not good enough, but you should give him a chance anyways."

"What?" I asked, confused.

"You would have normally talked about someone you were seeing or even work, so I'm guessing he's also on the team. I'm not excited about both of my girls dating football players, but there are good men out there."

"Thanks, Dad. I Love you," I said.

"I love you too," Soumaya said, coming back to hug both of us.

Dad chuckled and brought us in together for one big hug. "I love both my girls to the moon and back—no question about it."

15

LUTHER 'ZEUS' ZEUSES

I had heard through Coach Hobbs what happened with Zee. I don't give a fuck who you are or how good you are at your job—you don't treat anyone like that. It wasn't appropriate. I wanted to reach out to her the rest of the day. I thought about it throughout the entire night too.

Sunday three hours before Dom was supposed to pick me up, I sent a message to Zee, hoping I wasn't intruding in her day.

Zeus: Hey, I just wanted to check in with you after yesterday. How are you doing?

It had taken about fifteen minutes for her to text me back, but when she did, my muscles relaxed.

Zee: I'm okay. Thanks for checking in on me.

It had been short and simple, but she had responded. It gave me hope for her to come around to me.

I showered, jerked off, dressed in one of my finest suits. I looked pretty damn good if I did say so myself. Blue suit with a crisp white dress shirt. Brown dress shoes were the way to go, and just to pull it together, I added light blue dress socks with little mustaches on them. My lucky socks. We've won every game I've walked into the locker room wearing them.

97

I got a text notification on my phone a few minutes before Dom was supposed to pick me up.

Dom: I'm outside.

Zeus: Be right out.

Dom: Your hair is fine. Hurry up.

I chuckled and grabbed my coat. Double checking to make sure my door was locked, I walked out to his SVU and got in.

"I'm just going to say it..." he said.

"What?"

"We look good," he replied.

We did. I wasn't going to say it out loud, since he was already peacocking too much. This motherfucker had his girl and was still going the extra mile. I knew at that moment I was going to lose my best friend to this girl. He was hooked.

We parked in one of the closer parking garages about three blocks away from the actual gallery and walked there. A few people stopped us wanting to take selfies and get autographs. We'd never say no to fans. It can hurt us sometimes. Especially depending on if we've just started our night or if we were ending it. They'd post the photos on their social medias, and then we'd end up with a few more fans coming to get their own selfies. It can interrupt the evening, but it can also save it.

We watched as Soumaya and Zee got out of a Lyft and walked through the front doors. They were gorgeous ladies.

"Oh, man," Dom sighed, "why do I feel like a rookie about to get on the field for the first time?"

"Because it's real," I replied.

He swallowed hard. "You're not wrong."

Just as we got to the glass door, Soumaya was escorted off by a small group of other people. I watched as Zee looked around awkwardly for a moment until her eyes met mine through the door.

Her shy smile hit me right in the gut.

Dom opened the door, our tickets were scanned, and we continued through the velvet rope into the gallery.

"What are you doing here?" Zee asked.

Was she happy to see me? I was feeling pretty good at that moment. Had something changed? I had no clue, but I wasn't going to take it for granted.

"Dom was able to pull off a miracle and get us some tickets to support Soumaya."

That must have been a good response because her smile got even bigger.

"I thought it was sold out," she said.

"Apparently so, but Dom's got people. He's always getting tickets to sold out events."

"That's a good kind of friend to have."

"It can be. I prefer my friends being friends I can call on if I ever need to bury a body," I said then immediately regretted it.

She laughed though.

"You don't have to talk about it..." I said, letting the sentence hang for a second.

"Viktor was flat out disrespectful. It started nearly innocent. A lot of people don't know how to ask about heritage. But saying 'what are you' is bullshit," she said, covering her mouth and looking around to see if anyone heard her.

"You're good."

"But then he asked me if he could photograph me nude."

My blood boiled. I wanted to kill him. She could tell that my body had gone rigid and that I was fuming.

"It actually turned out really well. Bill—Mr. Conway spoke with him. He didn't deny any of it. At least that's what Jared said. Mr. Conway released him from his contract. Told him they don't work with anyone who doesn't agree with standard human decency."

"Good for them. Don't get me wrong... I was a little worried when I saw you leave and asked Coach what was going on."

"Oh, I actually left early because I had lunch with Sou and my dad."

"Oh?"

"Yeah, we do it a couple times a month, and honestly, I wasn't looking forward to it because of all of that. I wasn't in a good mental space to sit down with him."

"So, you didn't tell him what happened?" I asked.

"No. I only tell him things after there's an end. Otherwise, he'd be joining you burying the body."

I barked out a laugh just in time for Dom and Soumaya to join us.

"What's so funny?" Soumaya asked.

"We were just talking about burying the bodies," Zee replied.

Soumaya and Dom looked extremely confused. We quickly explained. It felt so natural to go back and forth with Zee, finishing each other's sentences and laughing about it as if it's been an inside joke for years.

They laughed along with us for a good minute.

"Okay, where did they put you?" Zee asked her sister. "Did you already find them?"

"We did," she said, pointing around the corner.

I leaned to see if I could see them from where we were standing.

"Oh, please, don't."

"Why not?" I asked.

"It's so strange having someone I know look at my art," she explained.

"Well, you don't really know me. So, we're good," I said, giving her a smile.

She covered her face in embarrassment. "Fine, they're over there," she said.

I held out my elbow for Zee to take. The moment her hand touched my skin, a burning heat rolled over my skin and coursed through my blood. I looked down into her eyes as she looked up into mine. A flash went off making me blink, and she looked away.

Fucking photographers. We were having a moment.

"Oh, these are Soumaya's," Zee said.

I was in awe. They were *passion* and *emotion*. I'd never really thought much about art, but everything about Soumaya's work hit me in the feels. Especially the red and gold piece with small details in black. All I knew was that I wanted it.

I hadn't wanted to stand there and purchase the painting in front of Zee or Soumaya, but I was going to get it one way or another.

"These are really great. I never really appreciated art before seeing these," I said.

"That was just what I was thinking. Everybody's work is really good. I wasn't sure what I was going to expect, but yeah, wow," Dom said, looking around and then staring straight into Soumaya's eyes as if she was the most magnificent woman in the world.

"You both are too kind. I'm still such a new artist. Some of these artists have been around for years, and their work has this classic, yet bold flare. I can only hope to aspire to have inspiration like them," Soumaya explained.

"I still think yours are the best ones here," Dom said, wrapping his arms around her from the side and kissing her rosy cheek.

I don't know how I could have possibly thought that Soumaya was Zee. They're completely different. Soumaya has a wild and free spirit. And there's nothing wrong with that, but Zee has this quiet, professionalism that gives her freedom. I think she's always allowed herself to be just there in the background so that Soumaya could shine in her own environment.

I watched as Zee smiled at her sister with pride. I couldn't take my eyes off Zee.

Their conversation blurred into the background as my mind went to ways I could make Zee smile at me like that. I'd take her in every way I could get her. In my bed, the couch, even the kitchen table. I wanted her in any and every way.

Casually clearing my throat, I said, "Excuse me, I'm going to go to the gents room."

I wanted to figure out who was in charge here. I was going to purchase the painting of Soumaya's that I loved. I checked over my shoulder to make sure they were still talking across the gallery.

"Do you know who I talk to about purchasing a piece?" I asked one of the caterers walking around with a tray of something that looked like crackers, tomato, and spit. Who the fuck would eat something like that?

"The desk," he said with an arrogant tone.

I looked over to the petite desk where a woman stood talking with a couple and looking through a massive spiral book in front of her.

"Thanks," I said over my shoulder, making my way away from him.

I waited behind the couple as they talked about payments and delivery arrangements. They had purchased two pieces. Neither was the one that I wanted.

"Thank you, Darling," the woman said to her husband.

"Anything for you," he said, looking at her admiringly.

"Can I help you?" the woman asked.

"I'd like to purchase one of the pieces," I said.

"Okay, which one?" she asked.

I didn't know how to tell her which one. "Over there. It's red and gold..."

"Name of the work?" she said, looking through her spiral notebook.

"I don't know. Oh, the artist is Soumaya Williams."

"That helps," she said with a smile.

She turned in her spiral book to Soumaya's work. Each one of her pieces was printed on its page with all the information available on the piece.

"Fierce. It's one of my favorites. Here is the total plus delivery charge. How will you be paying?" she said.

I didn't know exactly how these things were priced or how much Soumaya would get from the total purchase, but for five thousand dollars and then another five hundred for delivery, I wanted to make sure she'd get her worth.

"Card," I replied, pulling my wallet from my back pocket and handing her a black card. I was proud of getting a black card years ago. I never make a large purchase without it.

She processed the card, and I signed the slip.

"Thank you, Mr. Zeuses. When would you like to have the piece delivered? I've got openings every day this week," she asked, pointing at the calendar on her tablet.

It would take two whole weeks before I could get the painting. But it was completely worth it.

Any day could potentially work. I could have my housekeeper come by to sign off and accept it. She's been doing things like this for me for years. I made sure to schedule it and gave her my housekeeper's name to approve her as a possible recipient.

"Hey, what are you doing?" Dom asked, coming up behind me and putting his hand on my shoulder.

"Making a purchase," I said, smirking at him.

"What?" He chuckled.

"Yeah, I really loved one of her paintings."

His eyes lit up. "You did?"

"I did. Where are the girls?" I replied, looking around to find them.

"Soumaya is talking with another artist, and Zee needed to take a call," he explained.

"Where?"

"Over there somewhere."

I finally spotted her. She was pacing back and forth and talking on her phone. She looked nervous.

"You should go check on her. I think it was Conway."

ZERI WILLIAMS

started to get suspicious when Luther walked away to go to the restroom, but then Dom went to find him, and Soumaya got pulled away by another artist, and just as she was about to encourage me to come with her, my phone rang with a call from Bill Conway.

"I've got to take this. Go ahead," I said, shooing her away.

She mouthed the words, *okay, five minutes*, and held up her hand to represent the five minutes. She knew I would have a hard time keeping work to only five minutes. I had no doubt she would leave whoever she was talking with and come hunt me down to make sure I didn't work tonight.

I swiped my finger across the screen to answer it and walked off toward a corner with less people. "Hello?"

"Zeri, I need your help," Bill started. "We need another photographer, and none of them are available this week. We've been teasing the idea of new head shots and action shots for a full month."

"How can I help?" I asked.

"I trust you. Find me a photographer who can shoot it this week," Bill said.

"I don't really know sports photographers," I tried to explain.

"I just know you'll find the right person. Get me their information by Monday," he said.

"That's tomorrow."

"Then you'll have plenty of time. Thanks. I'll see you tomorrow," he said before he quickly hung up the phone on me.

I guess that's one way to get business done. Demand things be done or have the lingering possibility of being fired held over your head.

"Are you alright?" Luther asked, coming up behind me.

"Nothing." I breathed out.

"Something's up. Come on, aren't we friends?" he said, bumping his shoulder into mine. Well, it was more like his bicep than this shoulder.

"Bill wants me to find a photographer that can be there this week." I rubbed my forehead trying to stave off a headache.

"That's not a ton of time."

"It's zero time." I took another deep breath, unable to give myself a chance to come up with some obscure idea to save myself.

"What about your sister?" Luther asked, as if it was just that easy...

Could she? I mean he didn't say the photographer needed to have a studio. I know she's great at action photography, and she'd be able to get the exact photos I need for everyone's social media accounts.

"You're brilliant," I said, reaching to grab both sides of his chiseled jaw and pulled him down for a kiss.

His lips fused to mine. His hands wrapped around me. His fingers dug into my skin. I felt heat at my core. My body needed him with an intensity I couldn't explain.

I forced myself to pull away from him. For a brief moment, we stared directly into each other's eyes. His tongue moved over his lips.

"Wow," he breathed out. "That was..."

"A mistake," I said before he could say anything else then tried to walk out of the gallery.

"Where are you going?" he said, sounding confused.

He probably wasn't nearly as confused as I was. I wanted him. My entire body was demanding I stay with him.

"I just need to go," I said, looking around to see if a cab or Lyft was available.

"No," he gruffly said.

I spun around. "No?"

I saw it in his eyes. He knew he fucked up by telling me I couldn't leave. I watched him swallow hard.

"Talk to me, please."

I shivered in the cool night air and looked away from him.

"Here," he said, taking off his suit coat and wrapping it around me and pulling it closed.

I looked down and then up into his chocolate brown eyes. "This is a bad idea."

"What's a bad idea?" he whispered, getting closer to me and pulling me closer by his suit coat.

"This," I whispered back, my lips getting closer to his. "Let's go to my place." I put it out there before I had a chance to really think about the consequences.

He nodded. "There's a cab."

"Let's go," I whispered, huskily.

He lifted his hand, and the cab pulled over. He opened the cab door for me. When he got in, he looked at me.

"Where to?" the driver asked.

I rattled off the apartment building and street. I felt the car start to move and looked over at Luther. *What was I doing?* His hand came over and touched my knee. The warmth of his palm gently seated on my knee was perfect. I wanted him—needed him. There was no way I could walk away now. My body wasn't going to let me. My need for release was exceeding everything. I'd never felt this way before in my life.

The entire ride over, we hadn't said anything to each other. Perhaps too far gone to let fear take control of the inevitable pleasure that had been circling between us.

Luther paid the fee with a quick, "Thanks," and opened the door. His hand reached for mine and pulled me from the cab. Want and need bleeding through the cold of the night.

The cab pulled away as we walked toward my building. The silent walk to my apartment was nearly deafening as the clacks from my heels and claps from his dress shoes filled the halls. I unlocked my door. The door was just barely open when his hands found my body. We tumbled through the door, his lips finding mine as a frenzied desire took control.

His suit coat came off my shoulders. My fingers met the small buttons of his dress shirt as he pulled his tie free and tossed it. With his shirt pulled free from his dress pants, my fingers caressed the eight pack of abs that I'd been dreaming of licking. I dropped to my knees, kissing and nipping those God-given muscles along his chest and stomach until my eyes were at his crotch.

He had stopped and waited, watching me from above as I looked up and started to remove his leather belt.

His intake of breath told me everything—he hadn't expected any of this. I unbuttoned his pants and pulled them down his hips to his ankles. All that was left was his boxer briefs barely able to contain his massive erection. Need. Want. My fingers found the elastic of his waistband and pulled them down just enough to release the most beautiful cock I'd ever seen. The mushroom shaped head staring me straight on.

Opening my mouth, I leaned forward, engulfing just the head, licking an entire circle around his thickness and closing my lips around him.

"Oh, fuck." He groaned.

He was pleased. I looked up. He had tilted his head backward, and the slightest gap of his lips made me even more excited to give him a blowjob. His hand came to the side of my head as he looked down into my eyes.

"Take it," he ordered with a husky voice.

I pushed forward, taking more into my throat, the tip finding the back and making me gag ever so slightly. He flexed as my throat tightened around him. I started moving up and down over him. He held my head for a moment as I felt him get closer to orgasm, knowing he wanted to come down my throat. Barely able to breathe, my throat contracting around him as I gagged, and a pulsing from my core making me moan around his thick erection. The combination of all the sensations must have pushed him over the edge, and he came down my throat with a low grunt of pleasure.

I pushed back from him with my hands on his thighs and looked up at him. He tasted salty with just a hint of sweetness. Nothing like anything I've tasted before. It was the first time I'd let any of the men I'd been with come down my throat.

"I'm sorry, was that too much? I've been thinking about fucking your throat since I saw you," he said, looking ashamed and apologetic.

I enjoyed it. I had no reason to think he would have continued if I expressed any discomfort. There was an unspoken trust when it came to both of our sexual appetites.

"I'm good," I said, panting just a bit to catch my breath. I looked at his cock. Still feeling needy. He wasn't a one-pump-chump. Still hard and ready for more. "I really wanted it."

He breathed out a sigh of relief. "Please tell me if there is anything you ever don't like or want. I never want to take advantage of my position."

"What position?" I asked. Was he really thinking that he, Zeus Zeuses, was so famous that I wouldn't be able to tell him that I didn't want to have sex with him? I brought him to my place. There were clear expectations when I dropped to my knees.

"I mean, I'm pretty famous. People always recognize me."

"Alright, Mr. Big Shot," I teased.

His cock jumped.

I rose from my knees. "Oh? Did you like being called Mr. Big Shot?"

His cock jumped again.

"Maybe," he replied as I caressed and teased his body with my fingertips.

"Fuck me," I whispered, leaning into him and then looking up into his eyes.

"Yes, ma'am," he said just before his lips came down on mine.

I could feel as he stepped out of his dress pants I had left at his ankles and then he shimmied out of his boxer briefs. He gripped my little black dress in his fingers, bringing it upward, bunching it in his hands, and backing me toward the couch.

We weren't even going to make it to my room. This was going to be quick. The need we both felt wouldn't give us the time to walk any further. In seconds, he had my dress off me and on the floor. He flicked open the clasp of my bra, pulled it off of me, and tossed it over his shoulder. I heard it as it landed on the kitchen counter.

In front of the couch, he spun me around. My ass toward him, he bent me forward. My hands landed on the back of the couch.

I felt his hands move over my naked back to my panties. He gripped both sides and pulled them down. They laid at my knees on the couch.

His palms gripped my ass cheeks. As he spread them, he lined himself up with my opening. He thrust forward, impaling me, and pushing me forward with gusto as I let out a gasping moan of pleasure. He stretched me in all the best ways. It had been some time since I had been with anyone. My expectations were high.

"You feel so good," he said as he thrust in and pulled back out.

Tension was building as his balls slapped against my clit and his cock found the exact spot I needed to find my release. Higher and higher.

"I'm going to…" he said, giving me a warning.

"Keep going." I panted. My white knuckles gripped the back of the couch to keep me in the perfect position.

I felt it just as his cock thickened. My orgasm started, sending bursts of white light through my vision and a rush of pure pleasure throughout my entire body. Even my fingertips felt the orgasm.

"Coming," he announced with a groan.

"NO! NO! NO! NO! NO!" A familiar, exacerbated, pleading came from the door.

Soumaya and Dom were standing in the doorway. Soumaya was covering her eyes, and Dom was trying very hard just to look away and keep his composure. I covered what I could with my hands and rushed for the bathroom.

I was thankful when Luther and Dom finally left. I needed to talk to Soumaya and find out what her issue was to make her not jump at this insane opportunity. Forget nepotism, this was probably going to be the only time I'd ever be able to hire someone without five different people signing off. In this business, being the new kid in town was hard. Being unprepared is even harder. Since day one, I haven't been completely prepared. I've never been a huge sports fan. Why would I randomly know fifty-three players and all relevant people to the team? I don't even know where I'd find that.

The door closed, leaving Soumaya and me to talk.

17

LUTHER 'ZEUS' ZEUSES

It was beyond amazing. Everything was perfect. It was everything and more than I thought it was going to be. The entire ride home, all I could think about was how she felt wrapped around my cock. There couldn't be a better feeling in the world than how she felt. It was more magical than the first time I slid into Laura Jones in the seventh grade while her parents were at work one day after school.

Dom had been jealous at the time and has probably spent the last decade and a half trying to compete with the amount of women I get, but there's no competition. Having someone you can really connect with is truly what it's all about. I've been chasing some myth of the perfect woman, and it's been way too hard to find anyone who related with me. However, nothing is going to compete with Zee. She's feisty too.

I grabbed my loaf of bread, some SunButter and apricot jam to make myself a sandwich before I got ready for bed. If you haven't tried SunButter, it's definitely the best alternative for peanut butter. Plus grape jam is way over done. Strawberry isn't that far behind it either.

I got my sandwich made and cleaned up my mess. Getting a paper towel off the roll, I wrapped it around my sandwich and went up to my room. I set it on my bed and went to change out of my suit and take a shower.

I hung my suit coat on the hanger on my closet door and then tossed the rest of my clothes in the appropriate hampers for my housekeeper to take to the dry cleaner or do my laundry. Juliette was the best. She came by once a week to clean out my fridge, clean up my kitchen, do dishes and laundry, and dust and vacuum. I have her do all the stuff that I don't like to do.

I personally like being able to walk around my house free ballin' it. I walked into my bathroom to get my shower turned on. I had a full shower head system put in so that you don't ever have to think about whether or not facing the water is the best way to shower. I get a full three-sixty in water access. It's the best purchase I made, especially after games, to come home and stand in the heat for a good solid thirty minutes.

The moment the water hit my body, it was like a thousand little, tiny hands caressing me, including the mushroom tip, which was already sensitive from the round of fun I had with Zee.

Just thinking about her made my cock twitch and sprout to life. I palmed myself then rolled my fingers over the mush-roomed tip back and forth, creating suds and the perfect amount of *slip n' slide* for the release I needed by just thinking about her. The way she wrapped her mouth around me and then the way she clenched around me. The meat of her ass hitting my pelvic bone. I had gripped her ass and rammed into her with everything I had—and it was amazing as fuck.

Just like earlier, I found my pace and shot my load in the shower. Three releases in under twenty-four hours felt good. I'd been keeping my hands off as much as possible ever since my kiss with Zee, but feeling her entire body slap against mine will give me wanking material for the rest of my life. Her brown nipples and honey skin nearly did me in when she stripped down in front of me.

I got my loofa from the hook and finished cleaning myself

with my favorite body wash and then rinsed everything. Shutting off the water and then grabbing my towel I kept over the edge of the glass shower frame. I wrapped it around myself and stepped onto the gray bath mat. I walked out to my bed and picked up my SunButter sandwich to take a huge bite. It's so good after you let it sit for a few minutes. I'm also not picky about crumbs in the bed. You want Oreos at midnight after wild sex and a *Disney* movie—you got it. Crumbs are fine as long as I've got the girl of my dreams beside me.

In the morning, my day started out slow but the one constant—football. I don't think I've gone a day in the last two decades without picking up a football, and I had zero plans of stopping. I even have a football in my kitchen I play with when I'm making my protein shake before I go into practice.

I scooped the protein powder into my blender. I added my banana, oat milk, and honey to mix it all together. The whirring of the blender was the worst first thing in the morning, but I did it because these shakes were the best before practice.

I poured my shake into a blender travel cup and grabbed my keys to head to practice. I wanted to see Zee and talk to her about what happened between us. Because there was an *us,* and I was going to make sure she knew it.

I ended up bypassing a major accident and getting to practice a little early. I was going to try to sneak up to see Zee, but when I went through the office, Debbie told me that she wasn't in yet. Disappointed, I started to leave when Coach came up to me.

"Hey, Zeus, how's it hanging?"

"To the left," I quipped without even thinking about it.

"Ugh, don't make me give you lunges."

"You're the one who asked."

"I'm sorry that I did. I just wanted to know what you were doing up here."

"I was looking for Miss Williams," I said, pointing my thumb over my shoulder.

"Why do you need the new PR Manager? What the fuck did you do?"

Well, besides fucking the PR Manager, I'm kind of falling for her too. There was honestly no way for me to be able to tell him anything. Zee was right, our relationship was going to be hard.

"Uh... no, no problem. I just met her last night at the art show her sister had. You know she's dating Dom?"

"Zeri Williams is dating D'Angelo?"

"God, no!" I blurted out quickly. "Dom is dating Soumaya Williams, Zeri's sister."

"Well fuck. Okay, that's something I didn't know. So... when we were on the conference, the reason Zee was with Soumaya was because they're sisters?"

"Not just sisters—they're twins."

"Well fuck. Can you tell the difference between them?"

"Oh yeah. They're complete opposites."

"Really? My girls are a year apart, and sometimes I can't tell them apart," He explained, letting me in on a little of his family life.

Normally he doesn't bring up his girls at all. One just turned sixteen, so I'm guessing the other is about seventeen, and I think he's got an older daughter too. Maybe twenty or twenty-one. That's probably the real reason he doesn't bring them up here—they're dating age for a lot of the rookies. But hey, I can't say too much. I think I heard someone say she was young, and she's probably in her early twenties.

With a decade difference, you would think there wouldn't be that much in common, but I think I've got it figured out. When you grow up in a generation, you're literally growing up beside other kids your same age and you get to a point where there's just too much in common. I don't mind her being younger. She doesn't act younger. She's probably more mature than me on so many levels.

"Your girls are nearly at that college age, right?"

"No," He replied quicker than he needed to, then continued, "they're not ready to start picking schools or anything."

"Oh. Well, you should start convincing them now that schools close by are the way to go."

"That's not a bad idea. Thanks," he said as we started to walk away from the office.

"Didn't you need something from in there?" I asked.

"Nah, I'll deal with it later," he said but looked past me toward Debbie's desk and chewed on his lip.

"You sure?"

"Yeah, I'd rather wait to deal with it anyways," he said, patting me on the back to encourage me to continue walking with him.

"Well, whatever it is, I hope it doesn't have anything to do with me. I can't handle more shit on my plate than what's on it right now. I've got to focus."

"You sure do. Get ready and don't forget we're doing photos after our lunch break."

"What are we doing for lunch?"

"They're ordering boxes from Honey Baked Ham."

"Fuck yeah! I love that ham salad sandwich thing. Can I preorder like six of them?"

Coach laughed.

"I'm not joking. That shit is the best."

"I don't think they will stay good all week."

"I don't care; they are so good." I mimicked a chef's kiss.

He laughed. "I guess I'll have to try that one. I always get the roasted turkey."

"Never had it. Turkey makes me sleepy."

Coach stopped mid-step and eyed me. "You're fucking with me."

"Nope," I said, shaking my head from side to side. "Everyone says it. You heard it from nearly everyone at Thanksgiving."

"I don't even know what to say to that. Just go get ready for practice."

"Yes, sir," I said, saluting him and walking off with my shake in hand to go get changed for practice.

18

ZERI WILLIAMS

What the fuck? Not only does Dom lie about everything, but he's also got a baby? I knew I shouldn't have trusted him. I should have done my open research.

He set the car seat down outside his SUV and looked around for a moment. When our eyes connected, I narrowed my eyes on him. Why wouldn't I?

I got out of my car and started walking over to him. I was going to nail his ass to the wall. Soumaya wasn't going to want to be with someone who lied about having a baby.

"You've got to be kidding me. Don't tell me you knew about this and didn't tell Soumaya. This is definitely something she would have told me," I snapped at him the entire way as I came at him.

He fucking smiled at me. Okay, he was a dead man.

"What are you smiling at? This isn't funny," I said, sticking my finger into my face. I was going to aim for his chest, but I was furious on behalf of my sister.

"It is. This is Emmalynn... my niece. My sister was swamped, and I–"

"Oh God, you stole her?" I said with a gasp.

He snort-laughed. "No. Well, kinda. Dart and Rugby stole a bunch of apple cinnamon muffins then she had two wedding cakes and–"

"Who? What?"

"My sister owns *Sugar Mama's*. I went to get breakfast and her partner, Jen, she has these two huge German Shepards, Dart and Rugby. They stole the apple cinnamon muffins from the cooling rack. I offered to bring my very cold niece here, so they could get caught up. Does that make more sense?"

I was so confused. I slow-blinked as things started to register. "She did say something about you having a sister." I looked down at Emmalynn.

"Can you help?"

"Oh, yeah, of course... um..."

"The boxes?" he asked.

I looked at them with suspicion.

"My sister put together some pastries for breakfast to bribe them into letting her stay."

"Who's going to watch her?" I asked, taking the boxes and motioning with my head toward Emmalynn.

"I'm not a hundred percent sure yet..."

"I can." I quickly offered before I really thought about it. I had a ton of work to do and probably wouldn't be able to get much done with watching a baby. What was I doing?

"You?" he questioned, surprised, picking up the carrier and starting to follow behind me.

"And why not me?" I asked, definitely offended.

"Have you ever watched a baby?"

"Are you serious?" I deadpanned.

"Yes, you don't understand. I need a list of qualifications and references. Makenna would kill me if even one hair is out of place."

I chuckled. Also pretty sure I'd like his sister. "Okay, I get it. But I doubt that Debbie is going to be okay watching her while you're on the field."

He snickered.

Debbie Marshall was the only other woman in the office. She was a seventy-five-year-old executive assistant that basically runs everything. If Bill Conway had a new mole on his ass, Debbie Marshall would know about it. If she doesn't want you to get past her, then you never will. She's got it on lockdown, and I don't know why I didn't think I'd be able to sneak Emmalynn through her hawk eyes.

Also, she hates me. I don't even know why.

"Don't worry, you give her first pick of your breakfast bribe, and I'll sneak her past her desk," I said, failing to mention that she hated me.

"Deal." He handed me Emmalynn's car seat, and he took the boxes.

The little girl had remained asleep since I walked up on them and was yelling at Dom. All I had to do was get the sleeping baby past the gargoyle already at her desk.

Dom stepped up to her desk. She looked up seeing him walk in.

"Well, hi there, Dominic. How are you doing today?" Debbie said in a voice and tone I'd never once heard.

That bitch. She's never nice to anyone. What the fuck was that? That woman doesn't give anyone the time of day, and then Dom pops in there with sweet treats and she's like Mrs. Claus.

"Good morning, Mrs. Marshall. I'm doing really good. How are you?"

Yep, that's right. Debbie is married.

"Oh," she sighed, "I'd be a ton better if we didn't get a phone call from Viktor Cozcroft's lawyer."

"Oh?" he asked.

"It's this whole thing with Miss Williams. I don't get it."

Oh, that bitch. I narrowed my eyes.

I heard Dom clear his throat and looked over at him. He presented the pastry boxes to Debbie.

"I picked up some treats from my sister."

"Oh, Makenna? She's such a darling. How's she doing?"

"She's doing good. Getting lots of orders at Sugar Mama's."

"And how's that cute little baby of hers?"

"She's great," he replied, moving his hand behind his back and motioning with his hand for me to go past them. "Really getting into that baby lifestyle. Lots of baby talk. I swear the other day she said 'Unkie Dom' but I'm probably just imagining things."

Debbie giggled at Dom's absurdity.

I lowered down and started to sneak behind him as he continued talking to her. She had so much she wanted to say to him. I swear she typically tries to shoo me away before I can ask her a question. I bet she and the old PR Manager were besties.

I was almost there. Home free. I could see the finish line.

"WAAAAAAAAAHHHHH!"

"Son of a bitch," I said to myself.

"Who's there?" Debbie said, getting up from her ergonomic chair.

"Oh hey, Mrs. Marshall, it's just me," I said, moving so she could see me while I rocked the car seat with my foot trying to keep her from crying.

"What's going on over there?" Mrs. Marshall asked, adjusting her glasses on her nose.

"I stubbed my toe. Ow. It really hurts."

She looked me up and down. Then she did it one more time. I looked between her and Dom in hope that he could distract her long enough for me to get the baby into my office and out of range. I looked down. She was starting to move more. She was stretching and...

"WAAAAAAHHHHHH!"

"Is there a baby over there?" Mrs. Marshall hissed at me.

"Um, well..." I was floundering. I looked from her back to Dom and then back again.

"It's Emmalynn," Dom rushed to say. "Makenna was so

burnt out this morning that I offered to bring her with me. It wasn't until I got here and Ze–Miss Williams found me struggling that she offered to watch her while I'm on the field. I hope it's not an inconvenience on anyone since we're doing photos today."

There was no way she was going to accept that as a reasonable excuse. Not one way.

"Oh, that poor sister of yours. I'm sure she's feeling a little overwhelmed. And you're such a great brother for offering to watch her little one. Of course she can stay with us," Mrs. Marshall said.

Us? What. The. Actual. Fuck.

19

LUTHER 'ZEUS' ZEUSES

Zee came out with Soumaya to show her where to set up. I couldn't take my eyes off her the entire time. There was no way to mistake my girl between the two of them. She's everything. The way she came out so professional and strong. Zee didn't have anything to worry about strutting with her chunky heels through the crisp cut green on the field.

They stood with Coach Hobbs for a few minutes before Zee headed back into the building, but I caught her eye before she was too far away. She spent just as long watching me when she walked away as I had. I'd get her. I'd get her right after practice. I don't plan on letting her get too far once we're done here.

"You look like a man with a plan," Dom said, coming up next to me.

As soon as Zee was out of sight, I turned to catch Dom watching Soumaya as she got her tripod and camera set up at the other end of the field.

"Look who's talking," I said with a chuckle.

"She's everything. I think I'm going to ask her to–"

"Marry you?" I gasped out, interrupting him.

My boy was in love. I could see it on his face. He wasn't that far off, and I bet he's even really come to terms with the thought himself. Maybe he just doesn't know what to do with a forever girl.

"No!" he replied, affronted. "To come back to my place tonight."

"Is all you're looking for is a steady booty call for a few weeks, or is this something special?" I asked.

"No, I really like her."

"Then make some decisions and make sure it sticks. I think you and Soumaya could be a real thing. You've been different ever since you locked eyes with her."

"I know. She makes me want to be different."

"Oh? Okay, you're giving off major *As Good As It Gets* vibes."

"But I've got better hair than Jack Nicholson."

I barked out a laugh. "Leave Jack alone. He's got awesome hair."

He put his hands up and said, "I've got no beef with Jack. His hair is awesome. It's just that mine is better." He ran his hand through his hair as he looked over at his girl.

The man was the biggest flirt you could ever imagine. I know, I've seen it. He's gone through woman after woman with very little regard for the ones who actually liked him. In the end, it all turned out the same way. He ghosted each and every one of them. Trust me when I say that to truly ghost someone when your fans constantly post about you and your game schedule basically tells anyone who wants to know where you are all the time, it's tough.

I noticed Coach walking toward us. That was never a good thing. The scowl on his face was all I needed to know that we were about to get our asses chewed.

"I need to speak with the two of you," Coach said.

"What did we do?" Dom asked.

"What didn't you do?" he asked, eyeing us suspiciously.

"Didn't we already have this conversation?" I asked, scratching the back of my head.

"Yep, but since then, I've discovered interesting things."

"What would that be?" Dom asked.

"Well, that your fake girlfriend was just hired as the new photographer after the old photographer was fired because of the girl you're trying to get into bed. Who also happens to be your girlfriend's twin sister, who also happens to work for Bill Conway, and who also happens to be Zeri. Did I get all of that correct?"

I looked over at Dom when he looked over at me.

"No, no. You're not going to do that. I know exactly what's going on here. I had my suspicions when I found you lurking up in the head office, but they basically just confirmed everything I had thought."

Dom and I looked at each other one more time.

"Okay," I sighed, "we might have a confession we should mention."

"Uh-hm?" Coach said, crossing his arms over his chest.

"Dom here..."

"Nah, let me handle my own mess..." He paused to lick his lips. "I met Soumaya at my sister's house before Christmas through this really cool service called Retriever."

"Okay, I have heard of that."

"I signed up for the program to meet her again, but they were taking forever to approve me. Then that night, New Year's Eve, I saw her, but she didn't recognize me. It was Zeri not Soumaya. But I found Soumaya at Double Down and... yeah... I was just so excited about seeing her again that I might have taken advantage of the fact that I know the owner."

"Right, that's the club that Nix Drayden co-owns where you got caught with your pants down."

"Yeah, uh..."

"I kissed Zee that night. Then she ran off to find her sister—Soumaya. At the time we didn't know names or really anything else. Then we kind of just figured it out. You know, that they were twins and that we'd met them both on separate occasions."

"Did you sleep with her?" Coach asked, looking straight at me.

That really wasn't a good question for me to answer either way.

I started to open my mouth to speak, and honestly, I was going to lie...

"No, I don't want to hear any bullshit," he said, putting his hands on his hips and then looking over at Soumaya. "How'd this happen?"

Dom and I looked at each other one last time and then shrugged.

Coach stuck out his finger at me and snapped, "I know you. You're going to fuck it up, and then Zeri will quit. We can't afford to replace another PR Manager. There's not time. Especially with the legal shit revolving around your ass," Coach said, motioning to Dom.

"Me? What legal shit are they working on for me?" he questioned.

"Zeri's been working on the identity for our photo leaker, and she's putting together a lawsuit."

"She is?" Dom asked.

I knew he'd been worried about more photos getting out, even with the threat to the tabloids to pursue legal action against assholes who started all of it.

"Yes. Every day that woman comes into the office and is nearly a hundred percent dedicated to covering your ass. One hundred percent," Coach said.

I hadn't known that. My girl was working hard to cover my best friend's ass and his girl's. She was hot shit. I couldn't wait to sink inside of her. The only thing I had to figure out was how to get her back to my place so we could avoid interruption.

"Whatever happens here is going to determine a lot of the rest of the season. Don't fuck it up, or you might just not be here to fuck shit up next season," Coach said just before he walked away.

"Was that a threat?" Dom asked.

"Yup," I said, popping the *p*.

"Cool. Cool," Dom said as he looked over toward Soumaya again. "Hey buddy, I'll see you later. I'm gonna go see my girl."

He went straight over to Soumaya. The smile on his face was worth all the stress and frustration. He was in love. He pulled her close. She went up on her tiptoes, pressing her entire body into his, and he wrapped his arms around her, lifting her off of the ground ever so slightly then they kissed.

There was a bunch of hoots and clapping from our teammates once they noticed them with their full PDA in front of the entire team. That's one way to show Coach how invested he was with Soumaya.

When they pulled away from each other, you could see that they were both blushing. Soumaya buried her face in Dom's neck, and Dom called out to the rest of us, "Okay, okay. Knock it off!"

We all laughed and hooted some more. There was no way that Dom was getting out of this unscathed. We'd do our best to leave Soumaya alone. She looked like one of those girls who would be embarrassed easily.

"Come on, guys, let's leave them alone," I said, walking backward toward Dom and Soumaya.

"Are you jealous, Zeus?"

I was jealous. Dom was getting to be with Soumaya publicly. I wanted for Zee to be able to be with me—publicly.

I threw my middle finger up in response and heard a few chuckles from my caring teammates.

"Hey, Zeus,," Soumaya greeted me.

"Hey," I replied with a smile and leaned in to give her a hug.

"Hey, hey, she's mine," Dom said, working his hands in between us and pushing us away from each other.

I laughed. "No need for that. I'm after the one with the stick up her ass."

Soumaya snort-laughed. "I wouldn't say that, but you're not too far away."

"She's just stressing," I offered.

"She seemed fine this morning when she volunteered to watch Emmalynn," Dom said.

"Speaking of... you totally tricked Zee into watching your niece."

"No, I didn't."

"Oh, yeah, you did. You may not have realized it, but you totally did. It's like if a woman was out with her kids, not a single person would offer help, but if it was a man, there would be so many people helping him out. Poor baby, can't handle the kids without having a woman to save them," Soumaya teased, but it was an enlightening idea.

"Is that true? Does the dad always get people offering help and the mom doesn't?" I asked.

"Yes, did you hear about the family that was on the plane and the mom was denied a second drink, but the dad wasn't. When the mom asked why she was denied, the flight attendant replied that she needed to be able to watch her children."

"You're kidding me," Dom said.

"Nope. And the way you came in looking all *damsel in distress,* of course Zee's going to offer to help. Then, up there," she said pointing, "Debbie Bitch isn't even helping. Zee's got your niece, and it looks like she's had her the entire time. She was even mad when Zee asked her to watch her while she walked me out here."

"That figures," Dom mumbled.

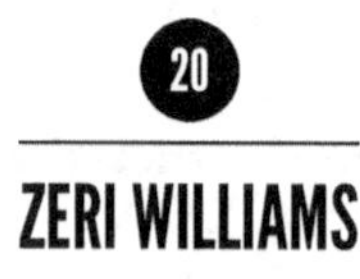

ZERI WILLIAMS

I wanted to drag Luther into a secluded place and let him fuck me like he had last night. It was the best sex I've had. I've only ever needed a little clitoral stimulation to reach orgasm. James definitely didn't do anything for me... speaking of...

I had Emmalynn in my arms, rocking her back and forth after her time with Debbie. She needed someone a bit more comforting. When I had walked back into the office, Emmalynn was wailing, and Debbie, bless her heart, was trying to comfort, but I think babies just know better.

"Shhhh. It's okay," I cooed, getting my cell phone from my desk.

I opened my message thread with James. He was really a bad lay. The last time we were together, I was making my to-do list in my head to get more vegan pancake mix and frozen blueberries. The orgasm wasn't worth the amount of secondhand sweat I had to wash off. Besides, he had probably gone off to fuck some other girl he was half-seeing and telling her she's not the only one either. I wanted to be somebody's only one.

Zee: We're not going to work anymore.

I didn't care that I was blowing him off over text. He sent

me a dick pic two weeks ago with another woman's panties on the floor beside his feet.

I also didn't expect a response. When those three little dots started moving, I was shocked.

James AKA Fuckboy: You're doing this through text message?

Zee: Yes.

James AKA Fuckboy: I had plans for us. I really thought we were going somewhere.

Zee: You're kidding, right? You've been seeing multiple other women.

James AKA Fuckboy: Can we at least fuck again?

Zee: No.

"We're just going to pretend that fuckboy doesn't exist. I might even take him off my numbers. Nobody needs someone like that on their body count," I said to little Emmalynn. "Good job, Zee, teaching her way too young. Oh my god, I'm going to be a horrible mom," I muttered to myself.

"I don't know if I would say that." The familiar voice of Bill Conway came from my office door.

"Bill, hi. I... um...."

He put his hand up to stop me from embarrassing myself more. "I've already heard this little jelly bean was here today. It's not the first time D'Angelo has done something like this."

"So I'm not the only gullible one around here?" I chortled.

He laughed. "No, you are, but I guess that's what happens being the rook and apparently the twin sister of the woman in the photograph."

The gig was up. "I was going to tell you. I just..."

"I get it. It better not happen again."

"I don't have another sister," I joked with him.

"I meant that you better not lie to me again," he said with a stern fatherly voice.

Heat rose into my cheeks. I was hiding something–Luther.

"What is it? Are you keeping something else from me? I

have to know. This is a multimillion dollar team. I can't afford anymore tabloid photos. This is already costing me thousands in legal fees and time to get dealt with."

"I should tell you…"

"Oh God, what?" He sighed.

I swear he was ten seconds away from clutching his left arm and toppling over onto my floor. If Bill Conway had a heart attack in my office, I would actually die. That's a lot of stress to put on a man in his almost seventies.

"Why don't we have a seat?" I said, nodding over toward the small sofa in my office since I had Emmalynn in my arms.

"Is it bad? You were supposed to make my life easier," he said as he went over to the sofa.

"It will all depend on how you react to this. Here, hold her," I said as I sat beside him and handed Emmalynn to him.

"Please, the suspense is killing me. Just rip the Band-Aid off."

"I'm kinda seeing Luther Zeuses."

He slow-blinked at me a couple of times before standing and pacing in front of me. It wasn't the pacing that was bothering me. It was the way he was trying to soothe Emmalynn when she didn't need to be soothed anymore.

"Bill?" I asked to get his attention.

"I'm thinking."

"Oh, okay," I said, leaning back and bringing my leg over my knee to cross my legs.

"When did this happen?" He stopped to question.

"Recently… very recently."

He picked up his pacing again. I decided to wait while he thought through what was on his mind.

"Let me get this straight; instead of doing your job on New Year's Eve, you brought your sister to the same club as more than half of my team. D'Angelo and your sister hooked up, and Zeuses and you hooked up." He looked at me very confused and slightly mad. "Was this job just about meeting a professional football player?"

"No! God no! I didn't have any desire for this to happen. Luther and I... he's really nice, and he challenges me. And to be honest, those boys were looking for trouble that night. We should be happy it wasn't with some gold digger."

He looked over at me like 'Come on'.

"I swear to you that Luther and I are taking this seriously," I said, hoping he felt the same way as I had after sleeping on what we had done. I was putting myself out there for Luther to toss away since we'd had sex. My job was on the line, not his.

"Zee," he sighed, "I'm going to set up a meeting with Diana in HR and Zeuses. Tomorrow. Be prepared," he said then he started to walk out of my office.

"Bill?" I questioned.

"Yes, Zee?" he said, sighing.

"The baby."

"Oh." He rushed back to hand Emmalynn to me. "Tomorrow."

"Tomorrow," I replied.

I spent the rest of my day with my anxiety at the edge, and all it would take was a feather to knock me off into the abyss. All I could do at this point was make sure Emmalynn was taken care of and find a time to talk to Luther at some point before tomorrow.

It was nearly time for practice to be over and Soumaya to be done for the day when Emmalynn started getting fussy.

"Is she getting hungry?" Debbie asked at my door. "Let me take her, and you can make a bottle."

That was a first. The only time Debbie helped was when Soumaya showed up and I had to ask her to take her and then my one and only trip to the bathroom. That was it. I'd take the opportunity to let her take her for a moment.

"I'm going to use the restroom as well," I said, handing Emmalynn to Debbie.

She huffed and took her from me. "You just better hurry. I don't want to be with her the rest of the day."

I nodded and grabbed the things I needed to make her a bottle and rushed off. It was better that I kept my mouth shut than to say something I'd regret, but I had wanted to tell her how the rest of the day was really only another fifteen minutes. I kept my mouth shut remembering the old saying, 'You catch more flies with honey than with vinegar.'

I went to the restroom first and then went into the communal kitchen to make her bottle. The moment I was done, I went to get Emmalynn from Debbie but nearly stopped in my tracks when I saw Dom coming in a few minutes early.

"Give it over," Mrs. Marshall said, holding her hand out for the bottle.

"Umm... okay," I said just as Dom walked in, making his presence known.

"Actually... I can take her," he volunteered. "When did she eat last?"

Dom looked at Mrs. Marshall; however, she didn't have an answer for him. When he looked over at me, I sighed and said, "Around one."

"Yeah, you're probably hungry, aren't you?" Dom said, taking Emmalynn from Mrs. Marshall.

"Are you done with photos for the day?" I asked.

"Yeah. Do you know what photo editing software Soumaya uses?"

"Oh, um... no, I'm not sure. It's on my laptop at home."

"I was afraid you were going to say that," he said as Emmalynn took her bottle and started sucking.

"Why?" I folded my arms protectively over my chest.

"I wanted to spend some time with her, but she just wants to get the editing done, and she doesn't think that you'll let her take your laptop to my house."

"Ah, I see."

"Hey there," Soumaya said from behind Dom. "Aww, aren't

you the most beautiful little peanut I've ever seen." She touched Emmalynn's little hand as Emmalynn wrapped her fingers around Soumaya's finger and then she looked up to Dom and said, "I'm guessing this is Emmalynn."

"Yes. Emmalynn this is Soumaya. She's very important to me," he explained.

Emmalynn giggled and cooed then squeezed Soumaya's finger just a little tighter. She probably liked her because she looked a lot like me.

"Did you need my laptop tonight?" I asked her.

"I'd like to keep up with the edits since it's a tight deadline, and I wanted to get back to Retriever duties."

"If you promise not to damage it, you can take it," I said. I knew I could trust her with the laptop. If she was that worried that she would break it, I knew she'd be so careful with it.

"So?" Dom asked.

"Yeah, fine. I'll go home and grab a change of clothes and the laptop and get a Lyft over," Soumaya replied, slightly rolling her eyes in annoyance.

"I can take you," I offered, thinking I could stop in at Luther's house and talk to him before tomorrow.

"I could come to your place," Dom offered, looking as though he felt bad for wanting Soumaya at his house instead of at our apartment. If he convinced her to let him come to the apartment, I wouldn't be able to talk to Luther face to face, and I needed to before tomorrow.

"No, that really wouldn't work," I said. "I'll just bring her. I've got some work to catch-up on and... whatever, I will just bring her." I tried not to sound too enthusiastic about needing to be in the gated neighborhood, but there really was no other option.

"I promise I will get my own car. I'll be able to once I'm done with this contract," Soumaya said.

Damn. I didn't want Soumaya to feel bad about me taking

her. I know she's been trying so hard to get caught up and match my own contributions to the apartment.

"I know. That's why I'm not worrying about taking you over to his house tonight."

"Alright, then it's settled," Dom said as Emmalynn finished sucking on her bottle. He brought her up to his shoulder to give her tummy time to digest and see if she needed to burp.

One of the largest belches came from Emmalynn. When he pulled her away from his chest, she looked worried.

We all laughed.

"You're okay," Dom comforted her, rubbing her back.

She quieted down and relaxed in his arms.

"Are you ready to leave?" Soumaya asked..

"Yep, let me just grab my stuff," I said, walking back toward my office.

I grabbed Emmalynn's car seat and bag then went back to get everyone set.

They stopped at Dom's SUV while I continued toward the car and said, "Hurry up so we can get home."

I'd have to grab some things. I wouldn't assume I would spend the night, but I wouldn't mind getting some more quality time with him. I've needed the release for months, and James was not making the cut.

I honked, watching them together. They were going to be apart for only a couple of hours. "Give it a freaking break," I muttered to myself and then honked the horn again. "Finally," I whispered as she started walking toward me.

"Sorry it took so long," Soumaya said getting into the car.

"It's fine. I just have some prep to do before tomorrow, and I wanted to make sure I had enough time to get it done," I explained.

"I can tell him we can't tonight. I don't want to get in the way."

"No," I rushed too fast to say, "I don't want to rock the boat. I'm already on the edge at work, and I think Conway isn't happy with the situation with you and Dom. We're still waiting on legal to get a response." I hated pushing that back on her, but she wouldn't argue since I was keeping her from public disgrace. Then again, her boobs are practically mine.

We parked and went up to our apartment.

"Let me just grab a change of clothes," she said.

"Perhaps you should grab a few days' worth," I said, trying to keep her up in her room a little longer so I could gather my own clothes without her discovery.

"Maybe," she replied as I heard her tossing around her things.

I rushed to my closet and picked out an outfit, business casual, for tomorrow and then rolled it as small as I could get it to put it inside my purse.

"Ready," she called out.

Most of the drive to Dominic's house we were talking about dinner with Mom and Dad. The fact that Dominic had answered Soumaya's phone to actually speak with our mom was stupid. Brave, but stupid. Now I'd end up sitting at the same dinner table with the two of them while our parents interrogated him for sport.

We pulled up to the gate. The same guy as before was there. As I rolled down my window, he smiled.

"Mr. D'Angelo said to go ahead and let you through."

"Thank you," I said from the open car window.

He nodded and opened the gate. We drove back toward Dominic's house. I already had Luther's address in my phone, so I knew which house was his.

He walked out from his house the second after Soumaya had texted him. Soumaya pulled out the small duffel bag she had packed for her overnight bag.

"This is it?" he asked.

"Yep," she replied, getting a laptop case from the back seat. "I'll bring it to you first thing when I get there."

"Please be careful with it. We can't afford to get a new one right now."

"Thanks, Zee, for dropping her off," Dominic said.

"Yep. No problem," I said with a wave then he wrapped an arm around Soumaya and led her toward the front door.

I started backing off his driveway and then went further into the neighborhood. I was a few blocks away and then pulled into Luther's drive. His house was beautiful. I loved the stone work on the front. I got out of my car and walked to the front door. Standing in front of the huge double door entrance, I nearly chickened out and went back to my car. Instead, I rang the doorbell and waited.

It felt like it took forever, but when the door opened, Luther was standing there with a smirk on his face.

"Well, well, well…"

LUTHER 'ZEUS' ZEUSES

It was late. Who in the hell was ringing my doorbell? I checked my doorbell camera and saw the only person that would make me open the door at this time of night. I swung open the door and met Zee standing there looking as if there was something she was about to blurt out and I needed to be prepared for it.

"Well, well, well, look at you."

"Can we talk?"

"How did you get in here?" I asked, crossing my arm over my chest.

I noticed her pupils dilate as she fixated on my biceps. I took the moment to look her over. She was wearing the same clothes from work with her peacoat over them. I'd watched her walk from one end of the field to the other while I drooled and daydreamed about everything I wanted to do to her.

"Through the gate. Can I come in?" she asked.

I moved out of the way and motioned for her to come inside. She strutted through my front door, unraveling her scarf from her neck and taking off her coat. I wanted her to continue stripping everything off, but by the way she requested we talk, I assumed there wasn't anything fun in my future.

"What's going on?" I asked as I closed the door and walked behind her.

"What are you wanting from this?" she asked, turning around to me.

"From what?" I asked.

"This. Us," she said, motioning back and forth between us.

Everything. I wanted everything. I take her to my bed and show her how much she was mine, but this was not a woman who could just be shown. She needed reassurance.

"Sit," I said.

She looked down at the couch beside her. I waited. She finally sat.

"Good girl," I said and then sat beside her. "What's going on?"

"I spoke with Conway today."

Well, that's one way to kill a boner. The big man. I honestly don't think he's ever liked me. Something about the fact that I was a 'signing bonus' for Dom. A few colleges were looking at me but nothing right out of high school. It was always Dom. He was recruited easily. And he was the one to have them give me a second look. It worked out great for them, and I've definitely earned it. Conway was happy with me as a rookie and for the last decade. We continue to renew my contract, but the newcomers are good—they're fast and agile.

"How'd that go?"

"I want to know what you want from us."

"Is that what he wants to know?"

"Yes. He wants to see us.

"Okay, well, I've wanted more since the night I met you."

"What's your definition of more?" she asked as she started to chew on her lower lip.

I pulled her lip from being chewed with my thumb. "More means more. We'd start out slow. Dinner, a few dates, spending the night with each other and doing all the things couples would do. Is that alright with you?"

The look on her face was everything.

"I told him we were seeing each other."

"Good."

"How is that good?"

"Because it's the truth. Conway hasn't ever really liked me much, but he likes you. Once he sees we're not making any issues for his team, he'll lighten up."

"Do you only want this so that Conway will like you?"

"No," I answered as quickly as possible. "This will always be about you and me first." I leaned in quickly to kiss her before she could spend too much time overthinking and drive away.

Her lips were soft and supple. She tasted like chocolate and coconut. She opened, letting me sneak my tongue inside and take the kiss deeper. I placed my hand to the side of her neck gently and then ran my hand around her back to pull her against my chest. She straddled my thighs and pulled at my tee I was wearing. I pulled it over my head to quicken our foreplay. I needed to be inside of her. She rocked her hips over my hardening cock.

"I need you." I breathed out, panting hard.

"Take me," she whispered near my ear.

I picked her up, my arms under her thighs and her arms around my neck. I wanted her bare breast against my skin. I took her upstairs to the master bedroom. She kissed across my jawline as I set her on my bed.

"You're wearing too many clothes," I said as I started unbuttoning her blouse.

"So are you," she responded, running her fingers over my abs and finding the strip of black hair that ran from my navel to my cock. "I love this."

She ran the back of her fingers up and down through the hair and then brought her lips to the spot and kissed.

She was driving me crazy. I was going to explode if I didn't get inside of her soon. I was going to spend the entire night making sure she understood exactly what I wanted from her.

I pulled her blouse off and tossed it to the edge of the bed. Then flicked open her light blue lacy bra so it would come off. It was the next to go. I wanted to spend time admiring her nipples this time. I regretted how I let myself be taken over by my urges. Zee's lips wrapped around my cock was the beginning of the end. There was no other way to end it last night than to fuck her. However, I didn't think I was going to get a second chance with her. It would be all about her. I secured my lips over one of her nipples. It hardened in my mouth as I swiped my tongue back and forth then swirled around her sensitive bud. Her back arched, and she opened her mouth with a silent gasp.

I maneuvered the clasp on her dress pants and started pulling them over her hips. She wiggled, making my teeth scratch against her nipple, and helped me strip her bare. She laid completely naked on my bed. I couldn't help but to take her in. The subtle differences from her sister in just her face would always be so obvious. This woman lying on my bed was mine. All the honey colored skin, chocolate nipples, and mesmerizing green-hazel eyes.

Mine.

I spread her thighs and ducked my head into her core. I rubbed my thumb over her slit. She was already wet for me. I plunged my tongue into her slit. My teeth nipped at her pussy. Her hands stretched out on my bed to grip the comforter with ecstasy. I found her clit and tortured the pleasure from her in the best way possible.

"Ahhhhh..." She moaned and twisted her hands in the comforter.

She tasted as sweet as she smelled. I could have feasted on her for the rest of my life, but I couldn't feast on her and fuck her at the same time. Either way, I was going to make my goddess orgasm on my tongue.

I inched two fingers inside of her and stroked her while I continued making her moan and writhe beneath me.

"Luther!" she called out as her pussy tightened around my fingers with pulsing contractions.

I licked up her juices and moved over her. "That was beautiful." I leaned over her and kissed her on her lips with her juices still on my lips.

She moved her hand over my bulge in my thin sweatpants. There was no boxer briefs on when I was at home. I could feel each finger as she passed over my tip and underneath side of my shaft. I growled low and deep from the back of my throat. It felt amazing having her hands on me. Fantasies had nothing on the real thing.

"Take them off," she demanded.

"You take them off of me," I commanded in return, standing up and giving her space to do as I wanted.

She watched me as I waited for her to come to me. When she finally gave in, she scooted from my bed and knelt on the floor.

"Good girl," I praised her.

The slightest smile gave me even more pleasure. She liked that I praised her for doing as I ordered.

As she pushed her fingers into the waist and pulled my sweatpants down over my hips, my cock jerked with excitement. I stepped out of my sweatpants once they were at my ankles.

"Take it in your hand."

She looked up from beneath her lashes where she remained on the floor. *I was a goner.* She wrapped her hand around my dick and stroked. Before I could pull her up from the floor and toss her back onto my bed, she engulfed my tip in her warm, wet mouth. I let my head fall backward. She was going to suck my cock if I didn't stop her. I would never refuse a blowjob, but I wanted inside of her. My hand came down to the back of her head as she sucked on me.

"Wait, wait, wait... I need to be inside you," I said, getting her to stop.

I pulled her up from the floor, bringing her closer to me and getting those perfect nipples against my chest. I kissed her again.

She melted into me as she relaxed and let me take over her body. I stepped forward, urging her to take a step back, and then took another step to get her back to my bed. She sat down on the mattress as I came up over her and positioned us onto the middle of the bed. I spread her legs apart and positioned myself even closer to her. Lined myself up and pushed forward.

"Luther!" She gasped.

I loved hearing my name on her lips.

I rolled my hips, making her purr. I thrust inside of her over and over, creating that perfect friction. I hiked her legs up higher over my shoulders as I thrust into her, nearly bending her in half.

"Oh God! Yes! Luther!"

That was all it took to push me over the edge. As the first contraction started to ripple around my cock, I felt my balls pull up and an overwhelming need for release. With a grunt, I filled her with my seed as she milked me dry.,

When we had both come down from our orgasms, I leaned back on my haunches giving her space to put her legs down while she caught her breath. I took the opportunity to look down at my cock to find it glistening with our combination of juices.

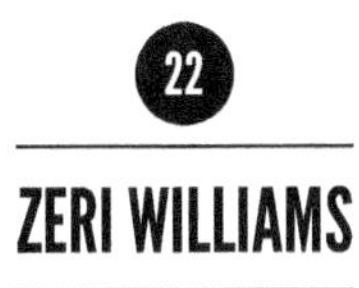

ZERI WILLIAMS

wo times now. He's been able to make me orgasm each time. There was no faking it when it came to Luther. He folded me like a pretzel and filled me. It might have also come to my attention while he was ordering me what to do that every time he said 'good girl' my core tightened with excitement, and I wanted more. Was this a new kink for me?

I looked him over from head to toe. His sweaty muscles, abs, and heavy panting made the butterflies in my stomach flutter like never before.

"Come shower with me," he said, moving to get off of his bed. His cock drug across the comforter as he stood.

Like I wasn't going to watch it. That thing could get its own zip code. He was massive in every way. And I had a massive *like* for him. He was smiling at me as I brought my eye back up to his eyes. Damn. I was caught.

"Sorry," I said apologetically and looked down.

"No, don't worry about it. I like that you're looking," he said, picking my chin up with his finger and making me meet his eyes again.

I got off the bed and followed him into his bathroom. The master bath was the same size as my room. A huge double vanity, toilet and bidet, and the shower—fuck me, it was huge. Probably a four by eight tile and glass shower with a whole shower system in it. My God, that was some money. I felt like I wasn't good enough for him. He was this famous linebacker for the Pittsburgh Scavengers.

"Are you okay?" he asked when I stopped in the door and didn't go any further.

"Your bathroom is huge," I said as I took another look around.

He chuckled. "Yeah, I'm not really a small guy, and my mom helped pick out everything, saying I was owed it. I grew up sharing a bathroom with her in our two bedroom/ one bath."

"I didn't realize—"

"I don't show or tell many people."

"Am I the exception?" I asked, looking up into his eyes.

"You're always going to be the exception," he said as he took my hand and led me over to the shower. "My mom wanted me to have this crazy ass shower with all the bells and whistles. The tiles heat up for those ice cold mornings before practice and when I need some more heat on my body. There's also the pulsing shower head," he said as he turned on the water for us.

I smirked. "You're pretty proud of that, are you?"

"Heck yeah! I earned everything in this house. Between torn muscles, sprains, broken fingers and ribs. Every pain was worth what I did for my mom and what I get to come home to. The only thing that's missing is someone to spend it with."

"You don't like the idea of screwing a different girl every night?" I felt self-conscious for the first time.

"I'm not going to lie to you. I've slept with a lot of women. But that's my past. I'm wanting this to be my present and future." He took my hand in his and brought it to his chest. Beneath his warm skin was a heart beating steady.

Luther might have been saying all the right things, but how was he going to feel in two weeks or even by the end of the week?

"There's no reason for you to be worried about what's going

on between us. This is happening. I wanted this from the moment you Cinderella'd me."

"I didn't." I mock-gasped.

"You did. You ran off and left me in your tracks. I went looking for you, but you were just gone."

"You went to find me?"

"I did, and I'd do it again."

"But you didn't find me. I found you."

He laughed. "You sure did, and you made me work for it."

"I don't think I made you work hard enough," I teased.

"You don't?" he said wrapping me up in his arms and pushing us both under the spray.

His lips landed against mine in a rush of passion. Water was cascading everywhere. Luther's hands were everywhere all at once. I leapt into his arms, wrapped my legs around his hips, and he pressed us against the shower wall.

Just barely bringing his lips away from mine, he said, "Can we fuck in my shower?"

I felt his cock come back to life and slap against my ass. Yes, please.

I nodded.

With a little adjustment, Luther reached down between us to line himself up with my opening. He pushed back in with one quick thrust. I wrapped my arms around his neck even tighter as he rocked us against the wall of his shower. He hit me in the most perfect spot while he fucked me. The friction made my clit sing out as another orgasm flooded my body and Luther's teeth bit at my neck and he spilled his juices inside of me.

Once we got out of the shower, he went over to his closet. "I might have something that could fit you. A tee? It's going to be huge on you."

"I actually brought a bag. It's in my car."

His smirk could have lit up the entire Midwest. "So you thought you were going to spend the night?"

"I didn't think I would, but if it was a possibility, I wanted to be prepared and not do the walk of shame tomorrow if you were interested in more," I explained.

"I'm glad you were wanting more, and I'm glad you came over. I'll go get your bag, but I've got to check on the game and see who won."

This time the smile on my face must have been bigger than his.

"What?" he asked.

"You're just really invested in the games."

"Well, yeah. We all are."

"Soumaya hasn't said anything about Dom interrupting their personal time for game scores."

"He's hiding it if he's not saying anything. I promised you I wasn't going to lie to you ever again. This is who I am."

"Okay."

"You'll stay here?" he asked, putting on sleep pants, and then grabbed a tee from his closet.

"Where would I go?"

He snickered. "I don't know. I kind of feel like this is a really good dream and I'm going to go outside and wake up from it."

"Nope, not a dream."

"Good," he said, then leaned over and kissed me quickly. "Where are your keys?"

"In my coat downstairs," I replied.

"Thanks."

I sat down on the edge of his bed in a towel and looked around his room. Lots of red and black. These had to be his favorite colors.

It took him a few minutes, but he was back in no time at all. I was debating whether or not to snoop further, but I decided to wait. I just wanted to know if I opened his nightstand if there was an opened box of condoms or some woman's panties... speaking of... where were mine?

He came back in with my large purse in his hand. "This was

the only bag. Is this all you brought?"

"Yep."

"I was looking for a bigger bag."

"Oh, I'm sorry. I um... I dropped Soumaya off, and I didn't want her to know I came straight here."

"Why not?"

"She's got enough she's been dealing with, and I've been kinda down on her relationship with Dom since the beginning."

"That's right, you really didn't want them to 'fake date', did you?"

"I didn't."

"Why not?"

"Lots of reasons. She's finally been responsible with her job, she's been helping with the bills more, and she's been getting serious about her art. I mean, you saw the art show. This was her third art show she's ever done, and she only does them when she's not seeing someone."

"Can you keep a secret from her?" he asked, handing me my bag.

"I can try..." I replied, suspiciously getting the small set of nightclothes out of my bag.

"It's not bad. I swear. I really loved her art. I actually purchased one of her pieces."

I froze in my search for a pair of panties. "You bought one of her paintings?"

"I did. I really liked it. You know the one with red and gold one with the black. I really loved it. *FOMO* was hitting me hard."

"FOMO?"

"Fear of missing out."

"I know what it means. I didn't expect you to ever feel FOMO or to say it."

We both laughed.

When it quieted down between the two of us, he looked into my eyes. Something about that moment and that gesture hit me straight into my soul. I sucked in a deep, shaky, audible breath.

"I had FOMO from the first moment I saw you."

I blew out air as I laughed. "You wouldn't have missed out. We just would have started this differently."

He laid back on his bed as I put my clothes on.

"How would we have started? Tell me the story."

"Well, we wouldn't have met in a nightclub."

"Where would we have met?"

"On the field," I said without any doubt.

"Oh, yeah?" he said, putting his hand behind his head and leaning on the massive headboard of his bed.

"Yeah, I would have been introduced to all of you knuckle-heads–" I watched as his smile widened across his entire face. "Hobbs would have told me all the gossip about who had the worst PR issues, and as I met everyone, you would have stuck out in the crowd, and eventually we would have met in my office."

"Eventually? I would have put the moves on you way before eventually," he said as he moved toward me, prowling like a panther slow and steady, ready to pounce at any moment.

"Eventually. We would have fought this between us for a while. Or as long as we could until I finally gave in to your advances and let you take me out on a date," I continued to explain as he took my hind in his and intertwined our fingers together. Taking an unsteady breath, I tried to keep going. "On our first date, we would have done dinner and drinks."

"And would I have convinced you to come back to my place?" he asked with a devious smirk on his face.

"Nope."

"No?" he questioned.

"I don't put out on a first date."

He chuckled. "I wouldn't be able to convince you at all?"

"Nope."

"How about in this reality? Can I convince you to come

back to my place?" he asked.

"You know... now that I've thought about it. We haven't even been on a first date. I should go," I said, starting to turn and walk away.

He grabbed onto me in play. I fought back while laughing, and then he picked me up and tossed me onto his bed. I was nearly cackling at this point as he came down over me and pressed his lips to mine. I was a goner.

23

LUTHER 'ZEUS' ZEUSES

Waking in the morning with Zee tucked into my side and her leg thrown over mine. I watched her sleep for just a moment before she started to move, and I let her. I didn't want her to know I was just watching her sleep, so I moved to get out of bed and go relieve myself.

I heard a noise at the bathroom door just as I flushed. I looked over to see her leaning against the doorframe.

"Good morning," I said.

"Good morning."

"How about you take your time up here getting ready, and I'll go make us some coffee and bacon and eggs?"

"Actually, I don't eat meat or dairy. Especially if I can avoid it."

"You don't eat meat," I said.

"I'll eat fish sometimes, but yeah, no meat."

"Okay. Umm..." My mind was going crazy trying to think of something I had in my house she could even eat.

"Don't worry about it. I've got a protein bar in my bag. Not everyone is prepared to be able to handle any kind of a restrictive diet."

I made the decision at that moment to make sure I had

150

things she could eat at my house. A few swaps for a more vegetarian lifestyle wouldn't hurt anyways. I already switched to almond milk for my after-workout protein shakes.

I'd have to talk with Soumaya about what I could stock my pantry and refrigerator with, everything she could eat. I wondered if Soumaya was also on the vegetarian side. Does Dom know?

"Does your sister—"

She cut me off, "No, Soumaya eats like a picky toddler. Lots of finger foods and nothing too fancy."

I chuckled. "Okay, so what are some of your favorite foods?"

"Well, mostly vegetarian dishes. Lots of oats and grains. Fresh fruits and vegetables."

I nodded. That was something I could totally handle... yeah. Doritos probably didn't count. Good thing when Dom told me to sign up for Retriever, I did it. I saw I was approved last week, and I was willing to have someone else make sure Zee felt at home in my home.

I'd get to practice today and talk to Dom about how this all worked and maybe even get a Retriever on my vegetarian grocery task.

"Good to know. I'll make sure you've got some options."

"You don't have to worry about that. I'm pretty used to having to eat around things since I'm the only one in the family. But my mom does make vegetarian dishes when I come for dinner."

"Well, I'm going to take it one step further. You're not going to have to search for something to eat when you're here. It's a priority now," I said as I walked toward her. "So, what are some of your favorite foods?"

"I like bell peppers and sweet peppers, pickles, and I love citrus fruits."

I loosely draped my arms around her, putting my body against hers, and patted her butt. "You will have all the snacky things you could ever want."

"You're sweet, but you really don't have to."

"I want to. That's the difference."

"Thank you."

"You're welcome." I leaned down and kissed her. "Shower and get ready."

"You don't want to join me?"

"God, that's tempting. But I'm going to fuck you in that shower if I join you, and then both of us will be late."

"Oh shit! Are we that close on time?"

"Yes and no. We'll need to beat some traffic. Go on." I kissed her quickly, turned her around toward my bathroom, and then spanked her on her ass to get her moving while I quickly ducked out of my room.

I went downstairs, putting together my shake in my blender and looking in the refrigerator for things that Zee would even eat. There was almost nothing. I had two big aluminum pans filled with chunked chicken breasts I had cooked on the grill, a bunch of lunch meat, cheese and condiments. I pulled my almond milk out and set it on the counter while I went into my pantry and looked around to do the same thing. All I found was a bag of old potatoes, and that was probably all she could eat. I grabbed my protein powder and went back out to mix my shake.

I wanted to give Zee her own personal space in my house so she could spend time in my space without me. I blended my shake and started pouring it into a shake container when she came walking down the stairs.

"You were quick," I said as I twisted the top onto my shake.

"Sharing space with someone your entire life makes you rush. We've always gotten ready together, and we've never had a ton of time to get ready because we're always in a rush."

"Good to know."

"Do you need to get ready?"

"Yep," I said as I put my shake on the island counter, kissed her on her cheek, and then hopped up the stairs. I'd shower at practice if I got a chance, but I didn't really mind giving her the time in the shower instead of me. I pulled my tee off over my head as soon as I got up the stairs, cutting an entire four seconds off my 'getting ready' time.

I went into my room and threw on the first thing I found to get out the door and then went right back downstairs.

"I can drive us."

"We probably shouldn't go in together. And I'll need to go back to my place tonight. Plus, Soumaya might end up needing a ride home."

"Okay. You wanna follow me?"

"Yep."

I walked her out to her car and gave her a kiss before closing her door and going to my SUV. I kept checking my rearview mirrors the entire way. In the parking lot, Zee had her own assigned parking space. I found one of the unassigned ones the players parked in and quickly pulled in so that I could get to her before she decided to walk in without me. We were doing this one way or another.

I opened her door for her so she could step out. As soon as she shut her door, I reached for her hand. The feeling of her hand in mine was exactly what I needed walking into another day on the field. I didn't see us making it to the super bowl this year, but we were still giving it a hundred and fifty percent. Our next game was actually Thursday, and I wanted Zee to be there—in my seats.

With her hand in mine, we made our way through the halls and up toward the head office. I knew Debbie Marshall would spread the word in no time.

"Oh, thank God you're here. I've been getting calls for you for the last hour," Debbie rushed to say and then looked between Zee and me before looking down at our hands. "They... they are calling about the *legal issue*." She whispered the last part.

"Okay, thank you," Zee said. "I'll call them back in my office."

I held onto her hand tighter and said, "I'll walk you to your door."

She scoffed. "You better get out there. You'll be late if you don't."

"Thirty more seconds won't hurt."

I walked her to her office, and just as I leaned in to kiss her, the phone in her office rang.

"That's for you!" Debbie called out.

"Thanks!" Zee said back. "Let me get that," she said, patting my chest and rushing to her phone. "Zeri Williams."

Her professional-take-no-bullshit attitude came out as she spoke. There was too little for me to actually understand what was happening, but Zee seemed pissed.

"No, that's not going to work. No. She will not do an interview with him. I'll speak to them about any other interviews."

That's my girl.

"No. That's not correct." A slight pause. "Okay, thank you."

She hung up her phone and turned to me with the biggest smile. She ran at me. I picked her up and spun around with her in her excitement.

"What just happened?" I asked.

"We won!"

"Won what?" I chuckled, setting her back down.

She adjusted her outfit and smiled. "Legal got everything they needed. They're settling with us. Dom and Soumaya are getting a payday, and they won't ever have to see any more photos or anything in the media."

"That's fantastic," I said, hugging her again.

"*And* the guy who sold the photo has charges pressed against him. He's going to be dealing with a huge legal battle."

"Now that's karma."

Her smile widened. "Exactly."

24

ZERI WILLIAMS

I sent Luther out to the team while I snuck looks out my window at the field. I couldn't help it. That man looked good in workout clothes. I could watch him every day running across that field.

I had worked the day on and off making sure social medias were up to date and no one put up anything vulgar over the weekend. I should have looked it over yesterday, but Emmalynn had most of my attention, and none of the players were being flagged in the media.

Andy loved putting selfies up when he's relaxing at home. He's got an entire album dedicated to outdoor activities. His swimming pool over the summer saw lots of barely clothed bodies. And he had this beautiful full grill and bar built where he does cooking all year around. It's the bare chest photos that keep sixty-eight percent of his followers female. The man's got some nice abs. It's just too bad his relationships don't last longer than a moon cycle. Poor guy needs to find a good woman that can not only keep his attention but can be very self-sufficient.

"Knock knock," Debbie said from the doorway.

I looked up to see her standing at the door very suspiciously.

"Can I help you?" I asked, putting my stylus down.

"Does Mr. Conway know about you and," she put her hand up to the side of her mouth and continued in a whisper, "Luther Zeuses?"

"Yes, Debbie, he does."

She eyed me with the grumpiest face she's ever given me. "Does he?"

"As I already answered—he does. Now, if you don't mind, I need to get back to work." I hoped she would just walk away, but she had to have the final word.

"I'm going to make sure he does."

I went back to work but remained frustrated the rest of the day with Debbie butting her nose in where it didn't belong. After social media accounts were approved for the week, I spent the rest of my day playing catch up and sending a kajillion emails and making sure I knew when everyone had vacation time over the off-season.

Soumaya had texted me in the middle of the day to let me know she was going to go home with Dom one more night. That worked for me. I'd go home and spend the night in my own bed and actually get some sleep. I did the mom thing and made sure she had clean underwear and that she was being safe. She assured me that she would be fine. I worried about the longevity of whatever it was happening between them.

My tablet pinged with an email notification from Conway. The subject line was the only thing in the email: 3:00 my office.

I knew I needed to set an alarm for it. There was no way I would be late for anything Bill Conway wanted. He could have been the most impatient man I've ever met. When he wanted something done, he wanted it done right then and there.

The moment my alarm went off, I started for Bill's office. His corner office overlooked the entire field and then some. That was an office with a view.

"Bill?" I asked from the open door.

He spun around in his huge leather office chair and motioned me in with the flick of a hand. Tentatively, I walked up to his desk and waited. I wasn't about to sit down without permission.

"Sit." He growled.

I sat in the chair on the right immediately. Conway continued to work. Silence. Pure awkward silence. All I could do was think of the fact that I needed something sweet to deal with all this stress. Soumaya had mentioned a couple of times about going to Sugar Mama's, and now that I know they accommodate for dietary restrictions, I was excited to see the menu. Perhaps I'd go after work.

I heard shuffling from behind. I tried so very hard not to turn around as I thought back to my third grade class when all the students were sitting around our teacher's chair as she read a story to us. Another teacher or maybe an administrator came into the room. We all turned around except for one student—Billie. After whoever it was had come in and interrupted, our teacher was disappointed with us for looking and then rewarded Billie for being the only one who hadn't looked. I won't ever forget that some things aren't any of my business. It didn't matter if someone important came into that office. I wasn't going to turn around for anything.

"Sit," Conway said again.

I felt him before I saw him.

"Yes, sir," Luther said as he leaned down, kissed me on my cheek, and then sat in the chair beside me.

"Yep, that's what we're here to talk about," Bill said, pointing his pen back and forth between us as he spoke. "When did this happen?"

"It—" Luther and I started at the same time. We laughed about the coincidence.

"It's been a couple of weeks," Luther said.

"That's all?" Conway asked.

"That's all," I replied.

"So, it's not serious?" Conway questioned.

"I wouldn't say that," Luther said, looking over at me. "We're exploring where this can go, and I think it's in a good place to go public."

"Really?" I asked.

"Yeah, I would say so, wouldn't you?" Luther asked, putting himself out there.

"I would."

I swear he was about to say 'good girl', which would have sent goosebumps down my arms.

"Bill?" Matthew Davis, head of human resources, said coming into the room.

"Yes, Matthew, thank you for joining us. You already know Luther, and this is Zeri Williams, our newest addition in the PR department."

I wanted to laugh. PR department? What a joke. It was just me and a guy named Craig that sent me a ton of emails and he scheduled things in the players' calendars. He did a lot to help, no matter how much he said he did or didn't do behind the scenes, and honestly I didn't even know who he was until the other day.

I stood to shake his hand.

"Good to meet you," he said.

"Same."

"Let's get this meeting started," Bill said.

"I thought it already was," Luther interjected.

"That was for my own personal knowledge. I'm not here to embarrass you or to call either of you out," Bill said.

"I'm here to make sure this relationship will not interfere with the rest of the season or the next," Matthew explained.

"Well, it won't," Luther said. "Are we done here?" He started to push up from the chair.

"It's not going to be that easy," Bill said. "I would like for the two of you to talk to Matthew about your relationship separately and make sure that your expectations are on the same page."

"Our expectations are on the same page. We both want to see where we can take it." He reached out with his hand for mine and intertwined our fingers.

"I want to see where this is going," I responded, looking from our hands together to his dark chocolate eyes.

Out of the corner of my eye, I caught Matthew and Bill eyeing each other.

"I don't believe our relationship needs to be called into question. The real question is will our relationship affect my job or the success of the team?" I said.

"I'd have to agree with that," Luther added. "There's no reason I can't have a relationship with Zee. I've checked my contract. I've talked with my agent. There isn't any policy that prohibits a relationship with anyone under the Scavenger pay."

He did research. I was not only impressed, but I didn't even have the foresight to look into my own contract.

"Correct, however, contract employees in the office have a different policy for a reason. If anything were to change between the two of you, then the success of the team could be in jeopardy," Matthew went on to state.

I felt a tightness on my fingers. He was gripping on to me for a lifeline, and I knew he was going to do something unexpected. I could feel it in my bones.

"Look..."

He was going to do it. I pleaded that it wouldn't affect my career.

"Zee and I are in a relationship. I didn't plan on it to happen, but it did. The fact is, at some point, I will retire, and I want a relationship and a family. I can see that future with Zee."

A future and a family.

Matthew and Bill talked for a moment while Luther and I stood out in the hall.

"What do you think?" he asked.

"I should have looked over my contract the moment he wanted to meet with both of us instead of going over to your house last night," I said, giving myself anxiety.

I felt his thumb tug at my bottom lip I was chewing on. Most of the time, I didn't notice when I started chewing on it. Sometimes my anxiety got so bad that I didn't even realize I was doing it.

"Don't worry," Luther said, trying to ease my nerves. "I enjoyed last night. I loved that you surprised me at my house and who cares about your contract."

"You're kidding, right? My contract is the only thing keeping a roof over my head right now. I love what I do. I don't want to lose my job–I can't."

"You won't lose your job. I think I saw something in Conway's eye when he saw us together. We're golden."

25

LUTHER 'ZEUS' ZEUSES

Was lying to your girl the best option when both of you basically just got called into the principal's office? No.

I'd rather make sure she was relaxed and not stressed about this. She was having such a great morning too. Getting Dom and Soumaya their win was so important. I wanted to take her out to celebrate her win. She didn't need this stress and reprimand. I worked best under those kinds of situations. I was pretty sure she was still unsure about where she stood in this world. She was good at her job, and she was good at everything else. I don't want her to feel unsure about us.

"You won't lose your job. I think I saw something in Conway's eye when he saw us together. We're golden."

She folded her arms across her chest protectively. I took a step closer to her and put my hand on her biceps and rubbed up and down until she took a step closer to me and pressed her body weight into me. I loved that she submitted to me for comfort, security, and reassurance. I've always wanted to be the one someone leaned on and needed.

The door opened abruptly, we both jerked our heads in

toward their direction, and Matthew motioned for us to go back into Conway's office.

"Come on, let's get it over with," I said.

We walked back into Conway's office. Zee seemed too nervous to sit back down. She acted as though she was ready to run for it.

"We've made a decision," Conway stated. "There's not going to be a decision."

My entire body felt like a boulder came off of my shoulders.

"What exactly does that mean?" Zee asked.

"It means we'd like for you to fill out some relationship paperwork that holds you responsible for your relationship and not the Scavengers."

"That's it?" Zee asked.

"For now. You're doing a great job, Miss Williams. We wouldn't want you to leave and find another team to work your PR magic with."

Thanks for making me feel like chopped liver. But I realized this wasn't about me. It was all about Zee. She was the real rockstar.

"I appreciate the compliment," Zee said.

"You're welcome. But I believe it's in the team's best interest to keep you around."

A slight blush rose into her cheeks.

"She is amazing, isn't she?"

"Very," Conway answered. "Matthew will email the papers to you, and I expect them back to him ASAP. Do you understand?"

"Completely," I replied.

"Yes, Sir," Zee said.

"Good," Conway said, shuffling papers around on his desk. "You may go. I'm sure you have something you should actually be doing."

"Yes, sir," we both said as we backed out of his office.

"Did we just get the go-ahead?" I asked.

"I think so," she replied, looking back at Conway's office.

"How about I take you out to celebrate?" I asked.

"I don't know if I want to take such a big chance so early. Especially with my twin and her photo still out there in the world. What if people think that I'm her and that I'm screwing both of you?"

A rumble started low in my throat. I hated that idea. I hated that she thought that would be something that would be spread around. And I hated that she was probably right.

"What if I took you somewhere where you won't have to worry about any of that?" I asked.

"Where?" she asked, suspiciously.

"I'd like to surprise you."

"I'm not big for surprises."

"I know. But this you'll like. I would bet on it the same as I just bet on us."

"Wow, that was kind of cheesy." She chuckled.

I laughed. "I heard it after I said it, but I don't have regrets."

We laughed together about it. This was what I wanted. I wanted someone I could laugh with and be myself. I couldn't just be the third wheel in Dom and Soumaya's relationship. Besides the fact that I already thought about Soumaya like a little sister.

"I'm glad, it was nearly worth it," she teased.

"Oh, yeah?" I grabbed her around the waist and brought her to me. "So, you'll let me surprise you?"

She sighed so deeply then said, "Fine."

"Okay, just save all that enthusiasm for my surprise."

She barked out a feminine laugh. "I will."

I leaned down and pressed my lips against hers. She gave me just a little bit more when she opened for me, letting me take our kiss deeper.

I opened my eyes as she started to pull away. Those green-hazel eyes could see into your soul. There was just something about her.

"I'll see you after. We'll go celebrate."

"Alright. You win."

"That's right and don't you forget it," I called out as I left the office to go back out to the field.

A few hours later, we were on our way in from the field, and most of us were just changing so we could get home to rest up for our game on Thursday. We anticipated we'd win it, but you never know.

I took the opportunity to shower and make sure I was smelling good. While I made sure I was afternoon date appropriate, I texted with Jen Brooks, my buddy, Ryan's wife, who works with Dom's sister, Makenna, on her delicious menu.

Zeus: Hey! I was wondering if you had a little time for me to come in today with my girlfriend. She's vegetarian, and I wanted to make sure we could celebrate without dietary issues.

Jen: Oh my gosh! A new girlfriend? We're excited to meet her and, of course, have plenty of options for her.

Zeus: Thanks! You're the best!

With my plan in motion, I made sure to take extra care as I groomed and got ready to meet Zee to celebrate her victory.

She met me at the door, ready to leave.

"Soumaya did decide to go back to Dom's house tonight."

"Do you want to come back to my place?"

"I could. I should get some clothes from my place."

"How about I take you to celebrate, and then I'll drop you back off here to get your car, run home, and then come back to my place, and I can show you just how much I enjoy making your toes curl," I whispered beside her ear so she'd be the only one to hear me.

A few of my teammates who hadn't left yet were still leaving and passing behind us as we talked.

"Are you sure that's not too much driving?"

"It's fine. I'd offer to take you home too just so I could spend more time with you, but I doubted you'd let that happen."

"You are correct. It shouldn't take too long. And I can be pretty quick."

"Alright. Then are you ready for your surprise?" I asked.

"I guess... unless you want to tell me."

I chuckled. "Nope."

"Fine," she said, perhaps a tad bit disappointed.

I chuckled again. "Come on. I promised you would love it."

I got her into the SUV and started on my way to Sugar Mama's—the best bakery in the world if I were the one handing out awards.

The moment I pulled into the parking lot, she started looking at all the marquees.

"Sugar Mama's? Are you freaking kidding me? Sugar Mama's? You took me to Sugar Mama's?"

I was starting to get nervous. Was she mad? I literally couldn't tell with her facing away from me as I parked.

"I did," I said cautiously.

"I just thought about this place today. Soumaya told me about it because they offer vegan options."

"That sounds like one hell of a coincidence. Dom's sister owns the place. I'm actually pretty good friends with her husband and the other woman that works here, Jen. I'm really good friends with her husband Ryan. He's a detective."

"So, you know the owners?"

"I do. And I called ahead to make sure there were plenty of options for you to celebrate properly."

"Really?"

"Yes."

She unbuckled, jumped to lean over the seat, and kissed me super quickly before turning and rushing out of the passenger side door. She was waiting at the front of my SUV while I got out and came around to her.

"You have no idea how exciting this is for me."

I opened the door for her, the bell going off over the door

and my two favorite bakers peeking out from the kitchen window.

"Hey Zeus!" they called out together.

"Oh my goodness! Is this the Soumaya?" Makenna said, coming around the corner looking between Zee and me. "What are you doing here with Zeus? Where's Dom?" she asked, looking around us for Dom.

"Makenna, this is Soumaya's sister..."

"Zeri–Zee. Call me Zee," she said, putting her hand out for Makenna to shake.

"Holy fudgesicles. You do look so much like Soumaya."

"We are twins."

"That's right. Dom said that. Well, welcome. Zeus was telling me you are a vegetarian."

"Yes," she said, shyly. "I can never find vegetarian or vegan options anywhere for sweets. At least none that taste good enough to want to eat again."

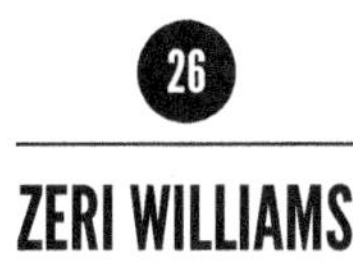

ZERI WILLIAMS

I couldn't believe it. I was standing in one of the only bakeries in the city that offered a vegan menu, and the owner was a family friend. I nearly came out of my skin with excitement. Seeing a non-cream cheese cream cheese on anything sweet made me want to cry with happiness.

"Come on in and sit anywhere. I'm Makenna, and this is Jen. We've got a whole tasting for you since this big guy is one, one, of our favorite customers and, two, told us you were celebrating. So what are we celebrating?"

"Oh, um... a legal win at work," I said.

"Are you a lawyer?" Jen asked.

"God no. I work in PR," I replied.

Makenna looked between me and Luther. "For the team?"

"Yeah, actually," I said.

"You're dealing with Dom's tabloid thing. Is that it? Are you celebrating that?" Makenna asked.

"Um... yeah. It's just not something I'm technically allowed to talk about."

"My lips are sealed," Makenna said.

"Mine too!" Jen called out while she gathered up a tray of

pastries and walked them out to us. "These are all vegan approved."

"Are you kidding me? That's amazing." I looked at a dozen different delicious treats on the tray. Two of everything.

"Yeah, we had to perfect a few of them over a couple of tries, but I think we finally got them the way we wanted," Makenna said.

"Yeah, they were kind of like the SunButter cookies," Jen replied.

"Right. Like those SunButter cookies Ronnie asked us to make for Blake," Makenna added.

"Right."

"Who is Ronnie and Blake?" I asked.

Jen and Makenna looked at each other and burst out laughing. "They are some good friends. She's a fun, kind of crazy–"

"Kind of?" Luther asked.

"Very crazy friend."

"Like crazy crazy?" I asked.

"No, not actually crazy. She's just super blunt and does things that might be considered crazy because she did them without thinking," Jen explained.

"Did?" I asked.

"Yeah, Ronnie and I both went through something pretty traumatic, and it's made her a little bit of a shut-in," Jen explained.

"That's sad to hear. I hope you both are starting to do better," I said.

"We are. It's just tough to get her out places."

"Maybe we can all get together. I can bring Soumaya," I offered.

"That might just make her come out of the house," Makenna said.

"It could," Jen said.

"You know, I like her," Makenna said to Luther.

"Me too," he said, looking straight into my eyes.

"I'm pretty fond of you."

"And that's our cue," Makenna said as she grabbed a couple of plates and set them in front of us. "What would you two like to drink?"

"What do you have on tap today?" Luther asked.

"A strong Venezuelan blend with hints of hazelnut."

"My favorite," Luther replied.

"I know. I put a small batch on just for you."

"You're an angel."

"Tell that to Mason," Makenna said.

"What'd he do?" Luther asked.

"He told me I was mean because I was so tired the other day and couldn't make him dinner. I made him order out."

I giggled. "Are you kidding me?"

"Nope, he's such a mama's boy. I think he'd be lost without me now."

Luther laughed. "He really would."

"Zee, what would you like to drink? Are you a coffee drinker? Or tea?"

"Tea. How'd you know?"

"Another one of our friends is a tea drinker. She absolutely hates anything coffee."

"Did she work in a coffee house?" I asked.

Makenna came over with two cups, one with a tea bag string hanging out the side and the other with a stirring stick. She set them down and tapped her nose. "You're right on the nose with that. Did you also work at a coffee house?"

"I did. But only for a few months. I couldn't handle how picky people were about their drinks."

"I know, right? Down to the number of..."

"Ice cubes," we said in unison and then laughed.

"Yes, well, this is a hot passion berry blend I mix myself and bag. We actually sell a lot of them by the bag," Makenna said.

I took a sip and nearly orgasmed. "Mmm. Oh my God, that's good."

She giggled. "Thanks. You should also try the sunrise blend. Jen made it. She loves citrus and raspberries."

"That sounds amazing."

"I think so," Jen said from the kitchen.

"I might just have to get both of those to take home," I said.

"I'll put you a sampler bag together as a gift."

"You are an angel."

Jen and Makenna laughed.

"What?" I asked.

"We just wouldn't call ourselves angels."

"I wouldn't either," Luther said with a chuckle.

"Don't make me take your sweets away," Makenna threatened.

"Okay, okay. Don't do that," he said, putting his hands up in the air.

"I'll run through what we've got for you two. Vegan raspberry mini cheesecakes with pistachio crumble crust, mini coconut cream pies, double chocolate fudge brownies, pumpkin cookies, almond butter oat bars, caramel apple cinnamon bites…"

As she went on, my mouth salivated. I wanted to dig into everything she put in front of us.

"You're going to have to wheel me out of here when I'm done. I'm not going to be able to walk, I'm going to be so full."

The girls giggled.

"That's what everyone says," Jen said.

"Which one do you want to try first?" Luther asked.

"I'm not sure. I think I'll close my eyes and just pick one," I answered.

I closed my eyes and circled my hand over the tray a few times before reaching down and plucking one up in my fingers. Opening my eyes, I saw the perfectly cut slice of peach.

I closed my mouth and brought it to my nose, inhaling deeply to bring the beautiful aroma into my lungs.

"Mmm." I hummed in enjoyment and then took a bite. "Oh

my God." I moaned. The more I let the creaminess of the lemon cream and the graham cracker crust with the peach fill my mouth, the more I knew I was tasting a masterpiece. "Oh my God!"

Jen and Makenna looked at each other and then at me. "We're so glad you like it."

"I don't just like it. I love it," I said.

Luther picked up the same kind as I had and popped the entire bite into his mouth and said, "That is good," with a full mouth.

The girls laughed at Luther's antics. Well, so did I. That was how the rest of our celebrating went too. Makenna and Jen were the best. I was really happy I got the chance to meet them, and I definitely wouldn't have minded getting together with all the girls. I already felt like I knew each one of them.

Makenna packed up the sweets we didn't get a chance to finish and threw in that sampler pack of teas for me. We said our goodbyes with hugs and promises to meet us soon with Soumaya and have a girls' night. Apparently, there would be eight of us in total if Soumaya and I were added to their group.

Luther took me back to my car, and he kissed me like a man starved for food. His lips melded to mine in the best possible way. I could kiss him forever and never be tired of it.

"Don't hurry, but hurry," he said, holding me in his muscular arms. "I don't want you to get any speeding tickets or into any accidents."

"My driving record is spotless," I replied.

"Then don't ruin it for me. I just can't wait to get you into my bed."

"You say that now…"

"I say that always." He leaned down to kiss me one last time so I could get going.

With traffic it took me longer to get home than I had wanted. But the moment I walked into the apartment, I realized it felt so empty. Soumaya was off with Dom, and I was spending more time with Luther. I hadn't expected for us to find two amazing men to want to spend so much time with so soon. I went into my bedroom to find my overnight bag. Something I could put a few more things in so no one questions us. I folded everything I wanted to bring and threw in a couple of pairs of shoes. I grabbed my toiletry bag to fill and everything else I needed to spend another night with Luther.

It was more than two hours later when I pulled up to the gate of his neighborhood. The same security guard came out and looked at me funny.

"Didn't you already go in?" he asked.

"My sister. We look a lot alike."

"You do. Are you going to Mr. D'Angelo's?"

"No. Luther Zeuses."

"Ah, that's right. He put someone on his list today. Where did I put that clipboard?" He finished turning around and looking for the clipboard.

"It's over there," I offered, pointing at the wall where the clipboard was hanging.

"Right. Can I see your ID?"

"Yep." I had it already out and ready.

"Thank you," he said, looking at my ID. "It says Zee Williams here."

"Yep, Zee is Zeri," I responded.

"I should call," he said, going back into the guard's shack.

"Of course."

Even with the inconvenience, I appreciated the security of him double checking. I wouldn't want anyone to be able to get through the gate with very little pushback.

It took a couple of minutes, but when he came back, he told me I would be good to go. He opened the gate and I drove through.

When I drove onto Luther's driveway, he was already outside waiting on me.

"What took so long?" he teased me.

"Traffic, getting organized, and the gate." I nodded toward the direction of the front of the neighborhood then gigot my overnight bag from the backseat.

"Let me grab that for you."

I handed my bag over, and we went inside.

"I have a surprise for you," he said, setting my bag on the sofa and leading me toward the kitchen.

"What's this?" I asked, looking at a full, beautiful vegetarian dinner at the table.

"I had some groceries delivered and maybe looked up some recipes and called Makenna to make sure I was doing everything right."

"You're the best," I said as I placed my hand on his chest and then kissed him. "This really is amazing of you. Nobody has ever done anything like this before."

"Isn't it time to start making sure things are done for you?" Luther asked.

"Yeah, it is," I said, pulling him to me and undoing the button on his pants.

I had plans for us. I wanted him to make me feel like a dirty girl. I inwardly groaned at my usage of 'dirty girl'. Even if it was in my head, never again I told myself.

"You are really amazing. But–"

"Oh-no, not the but."

I scoffed. "I was going to say, but I'd like to take you upstairs."

"Oh? I like that kind of but and your butt."

I snorted. "That was cheesy."

"I know, Tiger."

27

LUTHER 'ZEUS' ZEUSES

I spent the rest of the night showing Zee exactly how much I cared about her. Starting in the kitchen and ending in my bed. When we woke, I got ready beside her, and then we drove into 'work' together. It was everything I could ever want.

Soumaya took my action photos, and I loved them. She's such a talented artist. I was about two seconds away from telling her that I purchased one of her pieces of art, but then the entire day, I got caught up in getting invited over to Zee and Soumaya's parents' house. I was nervous and excited. It would be the first time I'd ever be meeting the parents.

———

As Dom pulled up behind their little car stopped in the middle of the road, I started to worry about Zee. She had already been stressed this week, and adding me as a surprise wasn't the best idea. There were a ton of hand gestures we could see through the back glass.

"What do you think they're talking about?" Dom asked.

"Us," I replied with any doubt.

The second after I said it, Zee jerked around and looked out the back window at us. Soumaya turned to look out the window right afterward.

"What do you want to do?" I asked him.

Dom picked up his phone and wiggled it between his fingers for them to see and hopefully realize he was going to call them. It rang once. Then twice.

"Hello?" Soumaya answered with a slight echo in the background. More than likely on speakerphone.

"Are you okay?"

"Yep. I told her Zeus was with you."

"I see. How is she handling it?"

"Not well," she answered.

My panic went through the roof. I didn't want her to be upset or worried about what her parents would think of me. Most of the time, the other players' mothers loved me. They thought of me as a big teddy bear.

"What's wrong, tiger? You knew this was going to happen eventually. Let's take a deep breath and just let it happen. They can't do or say anything that will change the way I'm feeling right now."

Zee nodded.

"Tiger, you've got to say it. Come on," I encouraged her.

I watched her through the back glass as she took a deep breath and then said, "We just need to do this."

"Good girl."

I could almost feel the tremor that went through her as I praised her for accepting the situation. I'd only done it during sex—or at least while we were headed in that direction. But to get a similar response from her for using 'good girl' was everything.

"Are we ready?" Dom asked.

"I'm ready. Are you?" Soumaya asked. She nodded once to reassure my girl.

"Ready," Zee answered.

Dom and I sighed in relief. Getting them to accept they couldn't control everything was huge. Especially for Zee. She was just one big control freak, and I loved it. Making her deal with the chaos of unpredictability was beautiful.

"Alright, let's go meet them," Dom said.

"The house is just up here on the right," Soumaya said.

"Okay, we'll follow you," Dom replied.

"Okay," Soumaya said just before hanging up with us.

They sat there a moment longer talking. I would have paid any amount in this world to know what they were talking about.

"What do you think they're talking about?" I asked Dom.

"Not a clue. But I'm a smart enough man to know not to ask," he said, looking over at me.

"Is that advice?"

"Definitely."

We saw them hug and hold on tight to each other for nearly a full minute. It looked as though they finally worked things out. When they pulled away from each other, Zee put her hands back onto the steering wheel and then brought the car out of park.

"See? All good," Dom said, sounding a little nervous himself.

"Yeah," I muttered.

Two minutes later, we were on the driveway. I looked up at the house as the sunset took over the night's sky and created a glow around the entire house. It was a small cottage with a clean yard for the winter season. You could tell they spend time on the landscaping. There was room in the flower bed for anything. My mom would love this place.

We opened Sou's SUV doors at the same time as the girls. We looked around at the exterior of the house. Dom walked over to Soumaya while I hesitated to get closer to Zee. She still looked very anxious, and I didn't want her to be overwhelmed by me beside her. I swear trying to figure out what she wanted was harder for me than anything. In the next fifty years, I don't think I'll ever be able to read her properly so I don't piss her off.

"How was that conversation?" Dom asked, putting his arms around his girl and letting her bury her face into his chest.

"Hard," she mumbled into his chest.

I was happy for my best friend. He found someone who needs him for the emotional support he gives. He's always been there for the people that mean something to him. He could have not reached out to his half-sister, Makenna, and that would have really changed the person he is.

We all heard the front door open, and then excited feminine squeals started and became louder as she got closer.

"My girls!" She squealed and pulled Soumaya away from Dom. "Where's your sister?" she asked, looking around. "Come over here."

Zee came over and joined in with the hug.

"You act like we never see each other," Zee said.

"It's not very often I can squeeze in a mid-week dinner. Especially since you've both been so busy. I want to hear all about your new job and your art show. How is everything go–" she said, cutting herself off when she looked behind them and then up. "Well, aren't the two of you..." she swallowed and fanned her face, "tall."

"Mom," Zee hissed. "Don't be embarrassing."

I smiled hugely. I liked her mom.

"What? I'm allowed to look."

"Not on my property." A tall man came up behind their mom.

"Dom, this is my mom and dad. Diane and Darrell Williams."

Dom stepped forward with his hand outstretched. "It's a pleasure to meet you."

"Same. It's very lovely to put a face to the voice," Diane said not letting go of Dom's hand.

"Mom?"

She still didn't let go.

"Mom, this is Zee's boyfriend, Zeus."

She jerked her head toward me, letting go of Dom's hand, and went to shake my hand.

"Hello." She put her hand in mine. Her eyes stayed locked on where our hands met. "Call me Diane. Both of you."

"Yeah, let's go inside before the neighbors see you two and we start a crowd."

Zee nodded in agreement. "Please."

Dom and I escorted Diane into the house. Both of us trying to make good impressions.

"Let's go ahead and sit. I made lasagna and a Mediterranean salad," Diane said as Dom led her to her chair. "Thank you."

"Have you girls been having a good week?" their dad asked.

"Yep, I finally got a media mess handled," Zee explained.

"Oh? Was it bad?" Diane asked, curious.

Zee looked between her mom, Dom, and then Soumaya. I knew what she was talking about. We'd received word that the lawsuit was in and that there was really good chances the media company would end up paying out and so would the guy that was paid for the photograph. Bill Conway had the best lawyers. Zee was ecstatic when she got the news yesterday.

"It wasn't horrible. It could have been worse. But we stopped the spread, and that's what's important."

"It is. Good job," Diane said so proudly.

Soumaya mouthed, *'thank you,'* looking at Zee.

"And Sou, how has your week been?" her dad asked.

"Good. I took the contract for the social media photos for the team, and the art show did great."

"Good for you. And Zee, why didn't you tell me about Zeus, was it? That's a peculiar name. Where does that come from?"

I looked at Zee and then back to her mom as she started serving our plates.

"Um, Zee and I are kind of a secret since I'm on the team and she works for the head office. At least keeping it quiet for now. We will go public at some point. As for Zeus, it's a nickname."

"Oh?" Diane asked, handing a huge plate to Dom and then asking for the next one to serve.

"Yeah, because of my size and everything, they took my last name and just shortened it."

"And what's your last name?" She asked.

"Zeuses."

Zee smiled at me.

"And your first name?" Diane asked.

"Luther," Zee and I said at the same time, looking at each other fondly.

"Look Darrell, how sweet are they?"

"They're sweet," her dad muttered, shoving a big bite of lasagna into his mouth. "What about you, Dom?"

"Sir?" Dom said.

"I was just curious why you felt you needed to defile my daughter in a nightclub?"

I wouldn't want to be in his position no matter what. At least when Zee and I fucked first, it was in her apartment. But I guess that's why he took her to a private area that shouldn't have been entered by non-employees. Even though he's not an employee, he knew the owner and the office owner.

"Dad," Soumaya pleaded for her dad to stop.

"No, I want to hear from Dominic," her father snapped.

"Sir, I know there's no excuse for what happened or how it happened, but if it hadn't happened exactly that way, we may not have had the opportunity to be here together."

The table was dead silent.

"But I thought you'd been seeing each other for a while?" her mom asked.

"We have," Soumaya was quick to answer.

Her father leaned back in his chair and crossed his arms over his chest. That's a fucking power move. Respect for the man for making sure his daughters were with a good guy. Even if

I could vouch for him, it wouldn't matter. Zee's dad doesn't know my character and doesn't know that I was in it for the long game.

"It doesn't sound like you have. How about you tell us the real story?" Her dad growled.

"We are—" Soumaya started.

"Okay," Dom started, looking at Soumaya, "I met Soumaya through Retriever when my sister needed someone to get her Christmas groceries when she was too busy. I went to my sister's house to meet the Retriever, who just happened to be Soumaya." He looked over at Soumaya again and smiled at her in reassurance. "I did everything I could to get a Retriever account as quickly as possible so I could see her again because I was too much of a chicken to ask her out. When I saw her at the nightclub on New Year's Eve, I was awestruck. I grabbed her and kissed her at midnight, and there's just no other way to say it than I'd been thinking about her for nearly two solid weeks, and I couldn't wait. I never meant for anything to be put into the public eye, but I'm in the public eye. Everything that happened was pure luck."

"And you don't mess with that," Soumaya added.

"No, you don't," he replied, leaning over to kiss her on her cheek.

"Now Darrell, you can't be mad at that. We knew our girls would fall in love with someone. Although I was under the impression that Zee was a lesbian. Who knew?" she said, shrugging.

"A lesbian?" Zee snapped.

I was taking a sip of water from my glass when she said it. I coughed, trying to clear my throat, but it went up my nose and touched the back of my throat, tickling the hell out of me and choking.

I felt Zee's hand sneak over and pat my back. When I cleared my throat, she rubbed circles on my back.

"We had considered it," her dad said, putting his hand over

Zee's on the table. "I was just seeing James. You both knew this."

"James? Who the fuck is James?" I snapped.

"It's not like we don't all have a past. James is part of it. Besides I know he was seeing other women while he was seeing me."

"Ugh, men are scum," Soumaya snapped.

"They really are," I responded. I wasn't going to argue with a table full of women and a father I was trying to impress.

Her mom giggled. "There's not a lot you can do for a man who doesn't want to be in a real relationship. When was your last real relationship, Zeus?"

I cleared his throat. "I went from being the tallest kid in our grade to the football player to playing in the NFL to help my mom. There wasn't really any time in there for serious relationships."

"And now there is?" her dad asked.

"I'd like for there to be. Now that I'm in my last few years with the team, I'd like to find someone to enjoy it with and start thinking about a family," I explained.

"And that could be Zee?" her mom asked.

"She's different than all the other girls I've met. She's beyond intelligent, selfless, and fucking organized. I love it."

Zee smiled at me and took my hand.

"Look Darrell," her mom said.

"I see it," her dad muttered. "So you two are good friends?"

"The best," Dom and I said at the same time.

"We've known each other since peewee. He's basically my brother from another mother," I explained.

"And our moms are really good friends," Dom added.

"Oh? What do your moms do for a living?" her mom asked.

"My mom is a florist," I said.

"And yours?"

"My mom is retired. She lives in Italy with her new husband on his vineyard," Dom said as he picked up his water to drink.

Everybody watched him. Silence around the table. Dom's not one of those rich kids that never worked for anything. He's not a prep school asshole, even if we went to a good school—thanks to his address.

"There's a lot to unpack there. Retired from what?" her mom asked.

"Umm... socializing. She did some fundraising for the country club."

"Alright, and Italy? That sounds lovely. What took her there?"

"She found out my father had an entire mother family and divorced him. Then went to Italy with Zeus's mom and found Vincent."

"Oh my," her mom said.

"Is it hot in here?" Dom asked, tugging at his collar.

"Let me get you another glass of water," Zee said, grabbing the glass and going into the kitchen.

"Another family? That's interesting. Are you in touch with any of them?" her mom asked.

"Yeah, my sister. We live in the same neighborhood now. I watch my niece a lot. At least when I can. She's a few years younger than me."

"Your niece?" she asked.

"My sister," he said as Zee handed him the glass of water.

"And Luther, how long has your mom been a florist?" her mom asked.

"Probably about a decade now. Once I bought her her dream house, she started a garden just as a hobby, and then neighbors and friends started asking her for her flowers, and it just turned into a business for her."

"How lovely. Does she still garden?"

"Yes, but not to the same degree. Her back has been hurting her lately, and she's decided to cut back on her variety. We actually just had a fountain installed where the bed was."

"I didn't know that," Dom said.

"Yeah, she likes to have a hot tea out on the patio some evenings."

"Oh, she does sound lovely. I bet we're going to be the best of friends," her mom said.

"I'm sure she would really enjoy meeting you. It's been awhile since she's been able to go out and have dinner with some girlfriends," I explained.

"That's so sad. Does your mom not come visit?" her mom asked.

"She does. A lot has changed in the last few years. She tries to come in on the off-season for about a month and then she comes in for either Thanksgiving or Christmas."

"Does she not do Thanksgiving with her husband's family?" she asked.

"Umm, they don't have a Thanksgiving the same way we do. Theirs is La Festa Del Ringraziamento. Festival of Thanks," he said, getting to use a little of the Italian he knows.

"So it's still Thanksgiving?" her father asked.

"Not really. Here we give thanks and remembrance of the Pilgrims and the Natives. In Italy it is more of a religious holiday about honoring patron saints."

"That's very interesting. Are you Italian?" her mom asked.

"I am. But not from Italy. I was born here and so were both of my parents."

"Ah," she replied.

"If you don't mind, I'd like to join you. You know, get a little fresh air," Dom said.

"Yeah, fine," Darrell muttered.

He stood so quickly from the table he nearly let the chair fall to the floor. "Sorry, excuse me," he said as he followed behind her dad.

Lucky bastard.

● **28**

ZERI WILLIAMS

I felt bad for Soumaya and Dom. The parentals were really tearing into them. Especially Dom. Dad probably was giving him the full ringer out there, and Soumaya kept looking over, perhaps checking to make sure Dom was still alive, and then back at dinner.

"Do you think he's okay?" Luther leaned over and asked quietly.

"Well, Dad doesn't have access to a shovel out there this late." Luther looked past my mom and back over at the door.

"Oh, stop. He'll be fine," Mom said, patting Luther's hand in reassurance.

I giggled.

"How do you know?" Luther asked.

"Because Darrell and I talked once when we found out we'd be having two beautiful girls, then when they turned thirteen and then again last night. Each one of those talks was about our girls finding someone who was good enough for them. We talked about what they'd be like and what they'd face as a couple. Your father is just putting that young man through the same torture your Papa Buster put your father through."

"Papa Buster?" Luther asked.

"Mom has the best story about how Papa Buster became Papa Buster," I said.

"How about you tell it this time?" Mom said.

I smiled and reached across the table for Soumaya's hand. "We both can."

Soumaya smiled at me and then took my hand. "Mom was in second grade when she helped make the second grade float for the fall festival."

"The trailer made it all around the city's center. It was even broadcasted on the local news," I added.

"When it was all done, all the floats came back to the high school parking lot and she was looking for her dad," Soumaya said.

"Did you find him?" Luther asked.

Mom nodded.

"She did," I said.

"He passed right by me. Didn't see me at all," Mom said.

"What? But you were what, like five or six? What did you do?" Luther asked, fully invested in the story.

"I called out *'Dad'* and he didn't turn around," Mom said.

"She started moving through the crowd of parents picking up their kids. When she turned around, she couldn't see the float or her teacher. None of the kids around her looked familiar."

"I called out *'Dad'* again and again and again."

"Did he hear you?" Luther asked.

"Nope," Soumaya said.

"So she called out…"

"Hey Buster!" we all said at the same time.

"He turned around and then she was found," Soumaya said, finishing the story.

"I ran over to him and wrapped my arms around him and he said…" Mom started.

"It's a good thing you called me Buster," the three of us said together.

"So his name isn't even Buster?" Luther asked.

"Nope, it's Joe," I said.

Luther laughed. "I think that's one of the best stories I've heard in a while. And you all call him Papa Buster now?"

"Yep. He's been Buster my entire life, and then when we found out I was pregnant and that he would be a grandfather, he said he was Papa Buster. It just always fits, and there's never been another name for him," Mom explained.

The back door slid open with Dad and Dom coming back inside. Dom leaned down and kissed Soumaya on her cheek before sitting down next to her.

"You two didn't stay out there long," Mom said.

"We had some things to discuss," Dad said.

Dom cleared his throat and picked up his glass. He probably put him under pressure outside and was still dealing with that conversation.

"Luther, how do you feel about children?"

"Mom!" I scolded.

What was that woman thinking? I pressed my fingers against my forehead.

Luther chuckled. "It's fine," he said, reassuring me by taking my hand. "I do want children. I just want to make sure it's with the right person."

"So you're not in a hurry?" Mom asked.

"I would be for the right girl. At least we would decide together when to start a family," he said, looking over at me.

"And how about you, Dom?" Mom said.

I tried to hide my wince, but Luther saw and held onto my hand a little tighter.

"One day," he said, then forked more lasagna into his mouth.

"How many would you like?" Mom asked.

Dom finished chewing and then swallowed in the most awkward silence ever.

"Mom, he doesn't have to answer that," Soumaya finally said.

"No, it's okay. I uh... I guess I'd talk with whoever I was married to, and we'd make that decision. I think people also change their minds depending on the situation."

"How so?" Dad asked.

"Well, my mom nearly died when I was born. She ended up having a hysterectomy, and I didn't get a brother or sister until I found out about my sister Makenna. But I was an adult when I found out."

The mood shifted at the table after that. Dom had said the perfect thing to get my parents to ease up on him and give him a little breathing room when it came to the interrogation.

"I'm sure that was very hard for your mother to go through. We were blessed with two at once, and I don't think I could have wanted it any other way," Mom said.

"That's true. Twins run in my family. There are several generations of twins on my side of the tree."

"Twins are a possibility?" Luther asked.

"Yep. The odds are much higher," I answered.

"That's kinda cool. I always wanted a brother. Dom's basically been that since we were little, but to be born with a best friend is pretty cool. I mean you've known each other since the womb," he explained.

"We have," Soumaya said, giving me a smile.

Dinner finally calmed down, and when it was time for us to drive back, Mom and Dad pulled me to the side for a moment.

"Do you like him?" Mom asked.

"Who? Luther?" I replied.

"No, Dom. For Soumaya. Do you like him?"

I looked over at Dom helping Soumaya put on her coat with a caring touch.

I nodded once. "Yeah, I do."

"And what do you think about your own date?"

"Luther? Yeah, I do like him."

"Good. I think they are very lovely gentlemen," Mom said, giving me a hug and kissing my cheek.

"You do?" I asked, really wanting her approval.

"I do," she said with a smile. "Don't hold back from him. He's a special one."

"Thanks, Mom."

"Anytime," She said and gave me another hug before going over to Soumaya to say goodbye.

"How'd that go?" Luther asked as he came up behind me and helped me into my own coat.

"I think it went really well actually."

He wrapped his arms around me and said, "Considering everything... I'm going to have to agree with you."

Luther walked me out to the car and opened the door for me. "Are you sure you don't want to come home with me tonight?"

"I'm sure. You've got a game tomorrow, and I'd rather you get a good night's sleep."

He pouted but only for a minute. "Fine. Tomorrow night. You and me at my place after we win."

"You're so sure of yourself, aren't you?"

"Definitely. I put your name on my seats."

"You know I get my own seats, right?"

"I know. I just want everyone to know that you're my woman."

I giggled. "You're so cheesy."

"And you love it," he stated so surely then kissed me. I opened to let him take the kiss deeper.

Someone cleared their throat behind us, interrupting our moment. I pulled away and looked behind me.

"We better get going," Soumaya said to me.

"Okay," I said with a sigh.

"Will you come to the game tomorrow?" Luther asked me.

"Are you asking me out on a date?" I teased him.

"Yeah, I am," he said with so much certainty there was no way I could turn him down. He wanted me to be there. Of course I'd be there.

"Will you both come?" Dom said as he wrapped his arms around Soumaya.

I looked over at Soumaya. She wanted to go. We'd never actually been to a NFL game. It'd be exciting to get to see them play.

"We'd love to," I said.

We said our goodnights and started our drive back to the apartment.

"I think tonight went well," I said.

"Yeah, me too. Even if it started out pretty awkward."

"Oh my God, I felt so bad for Dom. He was really put into the hot seat."

"He was, but he handled himself. I don't think he was really ready to meet the parents."

"I'd have to agree," I said. "How long do you think it will take for you to finish up the edits on the action photos?"

"The contract gave me five days."

"Only five?"

She sighed. "Yeah, I'll have to work hard over the weekend, and I'll have them sent in by Sunday night."

"I'll do what I can to help in the meantime."

"I could really use your laptop full time this weekend. Would that be okay?"

"Of course."

"Then next week, once the check clears, I'll go to the Microsoft store to pick out a laptop and then we can put a down payment on another car."

"What kind of car did you want to get?"

"Something cheap and reliable. Maybe a Honda."

I laughed. We'd talked about how reliable Hondas are over

and over, and she always disagreed and said she wanted something sportier. How the times have changed.

"Sounds like a good option," I said with a snicker.

"You're so mean sometimes."

"You mean when I'm right?"

"Yep."

29

LUTHER 'ZEUS' ZEUSES

I kept looking up to see if Zee was in one of my seats. It had been distracting me since we ran out onto the field.

"She's here," Dom said, coming up behind me and patting me on the back.

"Where?" I asked, looking around everywhere.

"Right there," he said, pointing.

There they both were. Our ladies. Zee looked amazing. Probably just came from the office and looked very professional. I couldn't wait to get her in private and strip her out of that so she could be my little tiger in bed. Soumaya was with Zee standing at the window of the private box and clapping. She blew a kiss down, and Dom caught it and brought it to his heart. What a goof.

The stadium started cheering, and I looked at the big screen. It was a split screen of Soumaya and Dom. The audio-visual guy must have gotten the go-ahead. A pink heart was around the two of them on the screen.

Dom winked and blew a kiss back at Soumaya, all completely one hundred percent caught on national TV—making them official.

Zee smiled and waved at me. I waved back, and then all the sudden, a renewed cheering took hold of the entire stadium.

Dom tapped me on the back of my shoulder. "I guess you aren't going to be able to keep your relationship a secret too much longer either."

There we were up on the same big screen as Dom and Soumaya. It took a moment for the stadium to calm and for us to get our heads back in the game, but by the time halftime came around, we were winning.

We had thirty seconds left on the clock. All we had to do was keep the ball away from the Aviators.

———

We walked off the field in great spirits. Another win for us. The team was in the locker room getting showered and cleaned up.

"You two made the game a hell of a lot more interesting," Andy said as he came out of the showers with a towel wrapped around his waist.

"It wasn't our intention," Dom replied.

"Doesn't matter. I bet there's going to be tons of coverage on it tonight," Andy said.

He wasn't wrong. It happened every time Andy was seen with a new girl. Would she be the next Mrs. Andy Barbarra? All inquiring minds wanted to know. Zee and Soumaya were about to go through the fire with our fans, and we couldn't do anything about it.

———

Outside the locker room, Soumaya and Zee were waiting for us. Dom smiled the moment he saw her and went straight for her.

"See you later, man."

"See ya," I said, completely distracted by the radiant beauty giving me one hell of a flirtatious smile. "Hey there."

"Hey. We made a pretty big spectacle of ourselves."

"I think it was perfect," I said, kissing her right on her lips.

"Perfect? More like extra work for me. We're already trending," she said, picking up her phone with a round of notifications.

I put my hand over her phone and gently pushed it down out of view. "Whatever happens will happen. It's just you and me tonight. Come back to my place."

She only paused for a second and then smiled. "I'd love to."

"You're not going to have to go home and get an overnight bag, are you?"

"No. I might have something in the car."

"That's exciting. Are you dropping Soumaya off at Dom's?"

"Oh, um… no, she has some work to get done and told Dom no distractions."

I chuckled. "I'm sure he hates that."

"I'm sure. But when Soumaya is committed to something, she will put all her energy into it to get it done. I really admire her for that."

"It's a good trait to have," I said as I took her hand in mine and we went out to her car to get her bag.

Dom was standing there with Soumaya trying to convince her to come home with him and not doing a very good job at it.

"Dom, leave her be. She's got work to get done, and you won't help her get it done at all," I said.

He frowned at me while Soumaya and Zee giggled.

"That's not fair–ganging up on me like that," Dom said.

"Fine, we're just here to get her bag, and we'll be on our way," I replied, looking in the car for her bag.

"I put it in the trunk," Zee said, going around to the back of the car and grabbing her bag. "I'll see you this weekend," she said to her sister.

"Yep. Thanks for letting me borrow your laptop again."

"Always," Zee said, giving her sister a hug, saying something to her and then coming back over to me.

Soumaya looked at me differently.

"What? What'd I do?" I asked.

"You bought my painting?" Soumaya asked.

Busted. "I did. I really loved it."

"I can't believe you were one of the ones who bought my art."

"Why not? You're really good at it."

She blushed. "Thank you, but you really didn't have to spend money on one. I would have printed you a copy of it."

"I didn't even think twice, and you should be paid for your work." I brought Zee into my side, looked down at her and said, "You shouldn't have told her I bought it."

"Why not? She'd find out eventually."

"Fine. I bought your art. I liked it."

Soumaya came running at me and wrapped her arms around my waist. "Thank you!"

I patted her on her shoulder and said, very awkwardly, "You're welcome."

Dom and Zee laughed.

Soumaya pulled away, glossiness to her eyes, as Dom pulled her to him.

"Can we go now?" I said out of the side of my mouth.

Zee snickered. "Fine, yeah, let's go. I'll see you later," she said to Soumaya and then we walked off to my SUV.

———

I pressed her against the wall as soon as we walked through the door. She opened the moment my lips touched hers.

I pulled her coat off, dropping it in the floor, and then went for her top. I was about to rip off the buttons to get to her bare skin faster. I didn't think she'd want me to ruin her clothes.

"I need you now." I breathed heavily.

"Your room," she said, matching me in need.

We dropped articles of clothes on our way, and just as she tossed her underwear, her phone rang.

"It might be Soumaya. Let me check really quick." She walked naked over to her bag and pulled out her phone. Her face changed completely. She put her phone back down.

"What's wrong?" I walked over to her, glancing at her phone to see what changed her mood so quickly.

James.

"Why is he calling you?" I asked, folding my arms across my chest.

"I don't know. I told him to stop."

Her phone stopped ringing but started up again.

"You might as well answer it and tell him to fuck off," I said, feeling jealous for the first time—ever.

Zee narrowed her eyes at me then answered her phone. "James, you have to stop."

"Put it on speakerphone."

She waved me off. "No. This is unacceptable. I told you no."

"Speakerphone," I repeated.

She rolled her eyes at me. "James, no, I don't want to—"

I grabbed the phone from her and put it on speaker.

This asshole was speaking some of the nastiest things I've ever heard.

"Listen up, you giant douchebag. She's not interested in your pencil dick, and you need to leave her alone before you have an entire army of lawyers sending you more paperwork than you can imagine."

The line was silent.

"Do you understand me, James?" I growled.

"I understand," he said very meekly and then hung up.

"I can't believe you just did that."

Was I in trouble? I was protecting her from that piece of shit.

"What?"

"I think he's finally going to back off," she said, jumping into my arms and kissing me with so much force that I had to take a couple of steps backward to catch myself. I walked her upstairs to the master, laid her down on the bed, and crawled over her while grinding my hips into hers.

She moaned into my mouth.

The last piece of clothing I still had on was my boxer briefs. She tried to work them off, but the way I had her legs wrapped around me made it hard for her. I slid my thumbs into them and wiggled them down my hips. My erection popped out ready to go and aimed right for the best place we'd ever been.

Stepping off the bed for only a moment so that I could push them down and then get back to what we were doing. She was up on her knees coming toward me. She pressed her body against mine at the same time she palmed my cock. I groaned as she ran her fingers over my tip.

"Lay down on the bed," she ordered.

"You don't have to tell me twice," I said excitedly as I hopped onto the bed and laid in the very center. She started at my feet and crawled toward me. Her hand wrapped around my cock and then she licked from base to tip. Her mouth was amazing. My cock couldn't have been any thicker when I pulled her toward me, kissed her until she was breathless, and then positioned her over my hips so she could ride me.

As she slid down my cock, her fingernails gripped my abs. When she was seated in position, I sat up to kiss her again before she started rocking her hips back and forth. Every side of my cock was rubbing against her walls creating the best feeling. If she continued, I was going to come quicker than she planned.

"You're going to make me come."

"That's the point," she teased.

"Is it?" I said, picking her up and putting her beneath me so I could get deeper leverage.

"Oh my God! YES!" she screamed.

I dug my toes into the comforter and picked up my pace. I

thrust into her as her pussy clenched around me with a vice grip.

"Oh God!" she called out, digging her fingernails into my shoulder and coming on my cock.

The extra wetness from her orgasm threw me over the edge. I felt it coming all the way from the top of my spine. It built and built until I felt my balls tighten as if it were like a cannon when I filled her with my release.

"Fuck!" I hissed out as the last pulses ebbed away.

I moved to lay beside her, put my arm over her, and within seconds I was asleep.

It was the best way to end the day after a win and the best way to wake up the next morning... and every morning after.

30

EPILOGUE: THREE MONTHS LATER

Zeri

"There they are!" Makenna called out as Soumaya and I walked into Sugar Mama's for an after-hours celebration with all our new friends, Makenna, Jen, Ronnie, Autumn, Brooklyn, and Chloe. They were the best group of women we'd ever met.

Jen and Ronnie had become ride or die girlfriends. Their husbands, Ryan and Blake, were detectives. Both overprotective, and they knew if their wives ever called needing a shovel and an alibi, they'd come up with one for each other. That's the kind of bitches we needed in our lives.

Autumn was super quiet, and even though Rocco, the guy who obviously was in love with her, tried to keep things professional, they would eventually get together. We could all see it. Makenna was like an amazing older sister from day one. Her husband Mason was coming to terms with trying to remember which one of us was which. Poor guy.

And then we met Brooklyn and Chloe. They'd been best

friends since they were little. Finding out Chloe married Brooklyn's brother made perfect sense. I had also known Nix Drayden through my profession. Of course, meeting him face to face when all the tabloid photo crap came out was a plus. And then there was Kane Winters, Brooklyn's husband—that man was beautiful and completely in love with her. There was also quite a cute bromance happening between Nix and Kane.

"What's everyone drinking?" Jen called out.

"You got Vodka?" Ronnie said.

"For you—yes," Jen replied.

I'm sure if Ronnie wanted to share with us the full story, she would, but I don't think she's even told anyone the full story. All I can say is that I'm fucking glad he's in prison. Brooklyn and Chloe were just the sweetest, and it seemed like almost everyone was trying to give Autumn some sort of advice so that Rocco would take the leap and give in to his desire—Autumn. We all saw it when he dropped her off.

We all ended up with a drink in hand and started chatting.

All the sudden, the only person that was heard was Brooklyn. "What's your favorite position?"

We all looked at each other, then Ronnie spoke up.

"I like when Blake uses his handcuffs."

"OOO, yeah, Ryan does this thing—"

"NO, NO, NO, NO!" Ronnie screamed. "NAHAHAHA-HAHA!" She stuck her fingers into her ears and closed her eyes.

We waited... after we laughed.

"Fine, okay. We like handcuffs too." Jen put her hands up in the air and continued, "That's all I'm saying."

"I like it doggy style," Brooklyn said.

"Nix does this thing—"

"NOPE! I know you have sex with my brother, and I love my nephew, but don't you dare tell me anything else."

These girls were close.

"Mason has this sailor's hat, and he ties a white handkerchief around his neck with the whole costume," Makenna explained. "Then I take him out to sea, and he–"

"Makes you wet," Ronnie finished.

Everyone giggled.

"Dom is–"

"NO!" Makenna and I yelled at the same time.

Everyone burst out laughing. I had a feeling they were all going to be my best friends.

We had our drinks in hand, talking about the best sex with our guys without saying too much because we all had limits, when Ronnie stood, thrust her pink drink into the air and shouted, "TO DICK!" and then threw back the last bit of pink drink in her glass and sat down.

It was going to be a good night.

Luther

I dropped Zee and Soumaya off at Sugar Mama's just after closing. Makenna suggested everyone get dropped off so no one would think Sugar Mama's was open late. Dom was at home preparing for a romantic evening at home. I told him she'd be smashed after spending the night out with the girls. But he wanted a romantic evening with just the two of them.

I pulled into the parking lot right at ten as discussed beforehand. There were two other vehicles already in the parking lot and two more behind me pulling in. I waved when I saw that one of them was my good friend Ryan. Kane, Mason, and Nix were already talking over by Mason's minivan. Ryan and I walked over to them. Blake was taking his time getting out of his vehicle. More than likely dealing with some important police business. We were just waiting for Rocco to show up. He's been circling Autumn for years, and now that she's living with him, helping him take care of his baby girl, we've been taking bets on when he'd finally make the move.

"What do you think is going on in there?" Nix asked.

"Nothing good," Mason replied.

"You don't think they're going to scare them off do you?" I asked.

"No, probably the opposite," Kane said. "Brooklyn and all her mothering is one of the sweetest women in the world. There's no way they're not falling for Zee and Soumaya."

Rocco pulled into the parking lot and parked beside us. "Sorry, I know I'm late."

"When are you not late?" Kane teased.

"Emilia was not having it."

"This is why I love Miss Kay. She's amazing."

"I know. Whenever Autumn has something she has to do, I almost always check to see if Miss Kay can help out. I'd give that woman all of my money if she'd leave you," Rocco joked.

Kane barked out a laugh.

"Are we ready?" Dom asked.

We all looked at our women inside Sugar Mama's, the heart and soul of us all, and couldn't imagine anything better.

The only thing we weren't prepared for was the conversation we walked in on. The bell on the door didn't even make a dint in the laughs as we all walked in.

"I don't think I'd ever use a cock ring on Kane."

"I think we want to try a butt plug," Ronnie said.

"Oh? A butt plug with the handcuffs maybe?" Jen said.

"Are you supposed to use department issued handcuffs for sex play?" Chloe asked.

"We don't. We have a separate pair for at home," Ronnie said.

Jen nodded as she brought her glass of whatever was pink up to her lips. Zee had the same pink drink, and so did Soumaya, Chloe, Autumn and Ronnie. Makenna and Brooklyn with clear drinks. Whelp, we knew who was pregnant.

"I don't think I've ever been this scared," Dom said.

The girls all spun toward us, rosy cheeks around the bunch, and they just stared at us like they'd been caught.

"I don't know about you, but I'm going to go home and get me some dick," Ronnie said then downed the rest of her drink as she stood and walked over to Blake, pressing her lips to Blake's and nearly swallowing him whole. When she pulled back, Blake's ears were bright red, and he had lipstick smudged across his lips.

"TO DICK!" they all shouted, raised their glasses, and toasted to our penises.

www.ingramcontent.com/pod-product-compliance
Lightning Source LLC
Chambersburg PA
CBHW052000150726
47999CB00004B/1462